The Belle Family Saga

The Pirate and the Belle
The Belles of Charleston
The Old Maids' Club
Carolina Girls

Other Books by Steve Brown

Black Fire
Radio Secrets
Hurricane Party
The Charleston Ripper

The Old Maids' Club

THE OLD MAIDS' CLUB

Steve Brown

Chick Springs Publishing
Taylors, South Carolina

Cover design by Heineman Design

First published in the USA in 2010 by
Chick Springs Publishing
PO Box 1130, Taylors, SC 29687
E-mail: ChickSprgs@aol.com
Web site: www.chicksprings.com

Library of Congress Control Number: 2010911808
Library of Congress Data Available

ISBN: 0-9712521-4-9
978-0-9712521-4-1

10 9 8 7 6 5 4 3 2 1

Author's Note

Acknowledgments

For their assistance in preparing this story, I would like to thank Phil Bunch, Mark Brown, Sonya Caldwell, Sally Heineman, Missy Johnson, Kate Lehman, Kimberly Medgyesy, Mary Jo Moore, Ann Patterson, Stacey Randall, Chris Roerden, Susan Snowden, Robin Smith, Helen Turnage, Dwight Watt, and, of course, Mary Ella.

For

A. V. Huff and Judith Bainbridge

Keeping alive the history of Greenville County

Cast of Characters

At Belles Lodging:

Helen, oldest sister
Mary Kate, middle
Margaret, youngest
John, only brother
Katie (Allison McKelvey)
Robert Patton, author
Eugene, hired man
Mark, soldier

The Laughlin Family:

Cleve, cousin of:
Andrew
Billy
Earl

From Charleston:

James Stuart, peddler
George Roper, mill owner
Fannie Archibald, George's mother-in-law
Samuel Roper, managing partner, Roper and Sons

The Lees of Ohio:

Edmund, husband
Victoria, wife
Betty Jean, daughter

And a deputy sheriff from Spartanburg County

"And when the quick have run away like pellets
Jack Satan smelts the dead to make new bullets."

—Ambrose Bierce

One

The attack on the carriage came from the ridge where three of the four men lay on their backs watching the clouds float by. All four men were drunk, and it was the fourth man, the one wearing a cowboy hat and returning from relieving himself, who saw the carriage and recognized the opportunity. A carriage filled with their most-hated rivals followed the winding road through the fall colors of an Indian summer, and that carriage was passing right below them. The mother and father sat in the driver's box and three children sat behind them, all singing songs they had sung at the revival earlier that afternoon.

Flaxen-haired Allison sat on the forward-facing seat at the rear of the carriage, clutching a picnic basket and laughing as she watched her older brothers tickle and pinch each other, sometimes laughing to the point of hysteria, sometimes forgetting the words of the song. At fourteen, Allison still worshiped the twins, followed them everywhere, and, of course, everywhere they went, the boys tried to leave their younger sister behind.

Why'd they even try? wondered Allison. She knew the farm, the barn, and the woods where the family's whiskey still was secluded as well as they did. No way her brothers would ever leave her behind.

When her mother realized the twins weren't singing, she reached back and thumped each boy's head with her thumb and forefinger. Since Allison saw this coming, it caused more laughing on her part. Properly upbraided, the children sat up and joined their parents in singing "Nearer My God to Thee" as the family carriage approached the single-lane bridge over the ravine. Below the bridge lay the river.

On the ridge above the carriage, the man wearing the cowboy hat harangued the other three to their feet and onto their horses. Once mounted, three of the four dug their heels into their horses' flanks and rode down the ridge. The last man, a redheaded man, could not calm his mount. He held onto the reins and chased his horse around and around in circles.

From the opposite direction came James Stuart, driving a covered wagon and heading for his next sales call. Though only nineteen, James had finally convinced his father to allow him to travel the upcountry alone. After all, it was 1915.

But James was no fool. A rifle leaned against his seat, a pistol was strapped to his hip, and a Bowie knife hung from the opposite side of his belt. And everyone knew the young man could use those weapons. During the years of traveling with his father, James had been the one to demonstrate the firearms.

He heard gunshots up ahead and guided the wagon off the road and into the bush. A nasty turn lay ahead where a bridge crossed a ravine; an excellent spot for an ambush. Pulling the wagon to a stop, James cocked his rifle, checked the load in his pistol, and made sure the Bowie knife was strapped to his hip. He'd never been ambushed, and James believed it was his reputation that kept bandits at bay. Or that he was a steady source of sugar for the whiskey stills in the coves and hollows of the foothills. Outsiders called this part of the state the Dark Corner.

James was tying up his horse when he heard the sounds of snapping wood and the screams of women. Keeping to the bush, James hurried forward and arrived at the curve in time to see several horsemen disappear on the far side of the bridge. He saw the break in the railing, then the horse and carriage in the stream below. The carriage was smashed beyond repair and the horse was struggling to free itself from its harness.

Those three, or was it four, horsemen had chased the carriage into the turn where the driver of the carriage had overcompensated, and before he could straighten out, the horse had driven through the railing and gone over the side and into the ravine below. It couldn't be anything but the result of an upcountry feud.

James took off his hat and wiped the sweat from his brow. After another glance at the far side, he slung his rifle over his shoulder, tightened the string on his slough hat, and started down the embankment. Halfway down, the vine snapped, and he lost his footing and tumbled into the water.

James struggled to the surface and swam into the

shallows. When he stood up, water poured off him, and he had to right his hat and the rifle across his back. He checked his pistol and knife, then slogged over to where the animal struggled in its harness. One of the horse's legs was broken, and a mother and two boys had been crushed to death under the carriage.

James turned away and puked. When he thought he had control of himself, he looked again. This second look caused him to develop a case of the dry heaves. Panting and red-faced, James remained bent over, watching the water rush between his legs and his sweat drip into the current. Straightening up, he wiped his face on his long-sleeved shirt and returned to where the horse thrashed around.

Need to get this over with and fast. Again, he checked the ravine and the bridge overhead.

Nobody up there, and it was about to become a bit too dark to find any other passengers. Spreading his feet, he took the head of the horse in his arms, calmed the animal, and slit its throat with the Bowie knife.

Once the horse quieted, James released its head, wiped the knife clean, and eased himself into the current, allowing the blood to wash away. When he surfaced, he found he had some assistance in locating one of the passengers. A voice came from downstream and sounded like a girl's.

Two

James stepped into the current and allowed the river to carry him downstream, where he found the father's body jammed under an outcropping of rock, face underwater. James grabbed the man's hair and lifted his head. Lawson McKelvey's head had been stoved in. Another victim of the Laughlin-McKelvey feud. The Laughlins were a Unionist family, the McKelveys former Confederates, and from time to time they'd have a go at each other even though the war had ended over fifty years ago.

He had seen the Laughlins and McKelveys having words last spring, but thought nothing of it. Laughlins and McKelveys had been having words since he'd known them, and as an outsider, he knew better than to meddle.

He left the dead man lodged under the rock, returned to the current, and allowed himself to be washed in the direction of the girl's screams. He found her around a bend and on the opposite side of the river, clutching a tree limb, a clump of yellow-white hair hanging in her face. Her dress clung to her thin frame.

James didn't believe she could see him with all that hair in her face, and she definitely wasn't going to let go of that tree limb. He learned that the hard way when he tried to grab her. The girl fought him off, causing James to lose his footing and slip into the pool of backwater under the limb.

"Girl," said James, after surfacing with water pouring off his hat, "you've got to let go of that limb."

She did, but when he grabbed her, the girl latched onto him so tightly they both went under. For a moment, it was all hands, elbows, and knees—in his face, chest, and several times his groin. The girl was determined to remain on the surface, even if that meant drowning James.

Remembering a trick he'd learned from swimming in Charleston Harbor, James went limp, and the girl realized she was on her own. She fought to stay on the surface, screaming, coughing, and reaching for the limb. James resurfaced, retching and coughing himself. When she reached for him again, James thought he was ready. He grabbed her hair; with his other hand he caught the limb and lifted her out of the water. As she came up coughing and flailing around, her hands hit the limb and she grabbed it and hung on. She peered at him through her blond hair.

"You want me to leave you out here?" he asked.

The girl let go with one hand and brushed the hair from her face, hooking the loose tresses behind her ears.

"You've got to turn your back on me so I can get my arm around you. If you don't, I'll leave you hanging out here until the beavers need that limb for their next dam."

The girl looked around. Plainly, she did not like her options.

"Listen to me, I've been to your farm before. I'm James Stuart from Charleston. What's your name? You're a McKelvey."

"Al . . . Allison."

"Well, Allison, your folks are upstream and you're downstream. What are you going to do about it?"

"Can they come get me?"

"Can they swim?"

She shook her head again. "We live up the hollow. There's only the creek."

"Then you've got to trust me."

Allison looked around for another option. She really didn't know this man.

"How old are you, Allison?"

"Four . . . fourteen."

"I remember. You were there when I sold that Spencer repeater to your father. You weren't large enough to raise it, but you tried."

The girl set her jaw. "My brothers don't like it, but I can lift it now. I just can't fire it without the recoil putting me on my butt."

James swallowed hard. "What are your brothers' names?"

"Thomas and Timothy."

"Well, your brothers are waiting upriver. You ready to go?"

The girl looked around. The sides of the ravine were steep, the current fast, and the backwater deep. Finally, she nodded, turned her back on him and let him wrap an arm under her chin. In this way, they crossed the river to the shallows and stood, dripping water. But James's problems weren't over. Allison saw her father under the overhang and splashed over to him. She grabbed his hair, raised his head, and screamed for him to wake up.

This went on for several minutes, and James found he couldn't reason with her. The girl simply would not stop screaming or trying to dislodge her father from the overhang.

He scanned the bridge and both sides of the ravine. How long before someone crossed that bridge, saw the break in the railing, and looked into the ravine? James understood these upcountry feuds, and it might be best that no one knew the girl was still alive. Even better if no one knew he'd been here.

"Allison!"

When she faced him, he popped her. The girl fell into him, unconscious; he slung her over his shoulder and slogged his way upstream.

At the dead horse and busted carriage, he found a necklace around the mother's neck, the Spencer rifle he'd sold the father, and an upended picnic basket racoons were getting into. Again, he scanned the ravine. It was making him nervous being down here so long.

Jerking the necklace from the dead woman's neck, he took a piece of railing from the bridge and jammed it into the throat of the dead horse to camouflage the cut made by the knife. Everything else he left as he found it, including the expensive rifle.

James was perspiring heavily by the time he reached a spot under the bridge used by fishermen. There, he stopped to catch his breath and untangle his hat again. The string had become twisted around his neck, his clothing leaked water, and his boots squished when he stepped onto the muddy spot under the bridge. Afraid if he sat down he might never get back to his feet, James refitted his hat on his head, the girl and his rifle over his shoulder, and leaned into the embankment, clawing his way up a crude path worn by fishermen.

At the top of the embankment, James stumbled to the road and stood in the bushes, listening. Sweat ran down his face, water dripped from him, and he struggled to bring his breathing under control. A late evening breeze snaked down the road, rattling dried leaves and knocking them to the ground. Indian summer was on its last legs, very much like him.

Satisfied that they were alone, James hiked down the road to his wagon. Opening the tarp covering the rear, he lowered the tailgate and laid out the girl. Climbing inside, he hauled the girl forward and positioned her lanky frame the length of a crate, but only after stripping her down to her petticoat and wrapping her in a blanket. Somewhere along the way, she had lost both of her shoes. Moving around, he collided with pots, pans, and ladles used to disguise the true nature of his sales calls. He was reaching for a bottle of whiskey when the girl regained consciousness.

Twisting off the cap, he handed the bottle to her. "Here, drink some of this. It'll help you sleep."

She did and didn't even make a face. By the time the horse and wagon had returned to the road, Allison was snoring.

Okay, the girl's safe. Now what?

Three

The Belles' house on West Washington Street had once been one of the social centers of Greenville, and for this reason the family had a reputation to maintain, even though circumstances forced them to take in boarders, traveling salesmen, and rich tourists from the low country. The homes were large, the yards narrow, and a few even had brick driveways leading to carriage houses.

By 1876, when the former Confederate States of America threw in their lot with the Hayes faction who promised that the federal government would end Reconstruction, the home on West Washington Street had evolved into Belles Lodging. Twenty-two years later, boosters led by Alester Furman button-holed committee members recommending where a new army training camp would be located. The boosters even traveled to Washington, where they received assurances from President McKinley that the new camp would indeed be established in Greenville.

Camp Wetherill, named for a local who died on San Juan Hill, was often visited by muckety-mucks from Washington, and naturally they heard of Belles Lodging. They were the first to refer to Belles Lodging as the Old Maids' Club, as no Federal, no matter how important, was welcomed at the house on West Washington Street. Later, the old maids even declined to take in rich tourists from the low country, as it was difficult to deal with those with whom you had once been social equals.

Margaret Belle met James at the rear of the house and pushed open the screened door of the back porch after flipping on an outside light.

That was luck, thought James. Helen Belle could be difficult and middle sister Mary Kate a bit pushy. Whenever James roomed here, Mary Kate would force her way into his room and attempt to matchmake. Mary Kate appeared to know every eligible young woman in Greenville County.

"Why, James," said Margaret, the youngest of the three sisters, "this is certainly a surprise. We don't usually see you until after Christmas." Though Margaret had recently turned sixty, her face held few lines and her hair not a touch of gray.

In the light, she could make out the wagon parked in front of the carriage house. "You haven't been in trouble with the law again, have you?"

Margaret was referring to James's tendency to take moonshine in trade for goods he sold from his wagon. Margaret knew one of the barrels on the side of the wagon contained sugar, but she had no idea a hidden compartment running the length and width of the wagon contained even more sugar. Revenuers were always on the lookout for those who made excessive purchases of sugar, and for this reason, the Stuarts could charge a premium for plain old sugar.

"No, ma'am," said James, clutching his slouch hat. "I have . . . well, there's a problem . . . with a girl."

Margaret's spine stiffened. "Then I can only suggest you beat a path to the justice of the peace and make the girl an honest woman. Unmarried couples are not allowed to reside under our roof, as you well know."

"It's . . . it's not like that."

An eyebrow arched. "Is the girl in the family way?"

"I don't think so." He could only point at the wagon. "She's in there."

"Whatever you're doing, pulling around to the rear of the house and coming to the back door, my sisters and I will have nothing to do with your shenanigans."

"Miss Belle, please—"

"Mr. Stuart, our home is no longer open to you. One of my sisters predicted you'd come to no good, and it appears she was correct. Now, be off with you before I send the hired man to fetch the police."

"Could you just take a look? Honest to God, Miss Belle, I don't know what to do with her. I gave her the last of the whiskey, but she could wake up any moment and start screaming again."

"Do not take the Lord's name in vain, James." She waved him off the steps. "Now be off with you." Margaret turned to go.

"But how do I get her out of my wagon?"

Letting the screened door slam behind her, Margaret flicked off the light. It was only when James added,

"The Laughlins will track her down and kill her" that Margaret Belle flipped the light back on and returned to the door.

"What'd you say?"

"It's a blood feud for sure."

Margaret wanted no part of any killing; the war had ruined her life and the lives of her sisters, so she hiked up her dress, pushed her way through the screened door, and strode down the steps and out to the wagon. As was her habit, she glanced in the direction of her neighbor's house. Mrs. Dutton was backlit in a window and staring at them. Margaret smiled and waved.

James untied the canvas covering the rear of the wagon and threw it over the top. Lying on a crate was a blond-headed girl who appeared to be sleeping, and snoring. Allison's head had rolled off the jacket James had placed under her and the blanket had become twisted, revealing the girl's legs with a hiked-up petticoat.

"James, do something about that!"

He scrambled up over the tailgate, knocking and rattling his way through pots, pans, and ladles, and rearranged the blanket.

"I'm . . . I'm sorry, Miss Belle." He returned to the ground. "My mother always said to get out of wet clothing before you caught your death."

Peering into the wagon, Margaret asked, "Where'd you say you found her?"

James squeezed his hat and stared at his boots. "I don't know if I should tell you. It might get you in trouble."

"Well, I can tell you that that child is not coming

into my home unless you can back her up with a good story."

Margaret glanced at the Dutton house and saw that her neighbor was still staring at them. The old maid peered into the wagon again. "She's not ill, is she, TB or the pox?"

"She didn't say."

"Well, this might be nineteen-fifteen, but we still . . ."

The screened door squeaked open, and Robert Patton stumbled down the steps and into the backyard. Patton, an author of stories of local interest, lived in one of the first-floor rooms and was usually involved in discussions at the dinner table. The topic for this evening had been whether the United States should go to war against Mexico over insults to America's honor. American troops already occupied Vera Cruz.

Patton took a cigar from his pocket. "Oh, there you are, Margaret. What are you doing out here?"

"I'm supervising the unloading of a package hauled all the way from Charleston."

"I'll be happy to help the boy unload it."

Margaret Belle thought there was little James Stuart could not do. Not only was he strong but quite able. "I can handle this, Robert, but I thank you for your concern."

Patton, ten years younger than Margaret, cocked his ear to the sound of the Crescent approaching Greenville. Its whistle was enough to get him hustling out to the street and down to the depot. Hardly any idler missed a train passing through. You never knew who might get off.

Once Patton disappeared around the corner of the

house, Margaret said, "Tell me all about it, James, and make it quick. People have finished with their supper and will naturally wish to stretch their legs."

James told her what he had seen and what he suspected.

Margaret listened closely. When the young man finished, she glanced at Dutton watching through the next-door window. "Now, listen carefully, and follow my instructions to the letter. This is what I want you to do."

Four

It was close to midnight when the Laughlin brothers and their cousin, Cleve, arrived at a roadhouse in Spartanburg County. Asked by a preacher why he didn't close down the roadhouse, the sheriff replied that he liked to have all the rascals in one place so he could keep an eye on them.

When the Laughlins came through the door, the room went quiet but for the squeal of a woman who had just been goosed by her date and the harmonica player who had his eyes closed as he played beside a young man strumming a guitar. The fiddle player reached over with his bow and tapped the harmonica player on the head. The far end of the bar gradually went quiet, patrons stopping what they were doing to stare at the four men.

Cleve, who wore a cowboy hat with a snake's head on the front, its skin forming the band around the hat, was the last through the door. He pushed his way past his cousins, Billy, Andrew, and Earl, and headed for the bar. There he was joined by a Spartanburg deputy, an angular, sunburned man.

"Gimme a beer!"

Cleve was a large, wide-shouldered man who owned a farm near Glassy Mountain, and revenuers knew he wasn't selling all the corn he grew there. It was rumored that Cleve operated a two-hundred-gallon still up one of the hollows, but no one ever mentioned Cleve's name, not unless he was on his deathbed.

His cousins studied the room before trailing him over to the bar. In the silence, Cleve looked the deputy up and down, noting that the deputy, as usual, wasn't armed.

Damn foolish, thought Cleve. You always brought along a pistol when visiting any roadhouse. Of course, Cleve was willing to yield on the point that he might have a few more enemies than this here deputy.

He noticed the bartender hadn't set up his beer. Cleve looked around. People stood on the dance floor, not moving.

A mechanic who liked to brag about all the cars he had worked on, from Studebakers to the Stanley Steamer, returned from the outhouse. Coming through the door while buttoning his fly, he noticed the quiet and stepped behind a group of smokers to finish buttoning his fly.

"My money no good in this place?" Cleve asked the bartender.

"That's right," said the deputy, tossing some currency on the bar and jerking his thumb at Cleve's cousins. "Give them their usual." He slapped Cleve on the shoulder and steered him away from the bar and toward a door at the end of the bar. "Bring the drinks in there."

Cleve glanced over his shoulder, saw his cousins trailing along, and went through the door opened by the deputy.

The adjoining room was much smaller, thick with smoke, and sported a table with five card players. A brunette in a sleeveless dress sat in the lap of one of the players. Her hair was piled high and she wore bright red lipstick.

The deputy motioned the four Laughlins to a table used for blackjack and took the seat reserved for the dealer, his back to the wall. The bartender followed them into the room and placed three bottles of beer and two bottles of Coca-Cola on the table. Redheaded Earl and the Spartanburg deputy were known as Coca-Cola drinkers.

Once the bartender left the smaller room, the deputy asked, "So, they wouldn't let you in a bar in Greenville County tonight?"

"We didn't even try." Cleve downed a good bit of his beer, then leaned back and pulled a cigar from his coat pocket.

"What's the use," said Billy Laughlin, a dark-skinned, black-haired fellow. "You saw how they treated us at the bridge, and we was only there to help."

Even in the darkness, someone had noticed the break in the bridge railing, then, by flashlight, the carriage and dead horse in the ravine below. It wasn't long before the call went out, not only for the sheriff, but anyone with a rope. There were quite a few, some with chains. By nine four bodies had been recovered and the busted carriage and dead horse had been hoisted up the side of the ravine. Others, using flashlights, searched downstream for the missing girl. The Greenville County sheriff was confident that they would find her. Still, by midnight when the search party called it a day, the girl's body had yet to be recovered.

Billy's comment referred to the cold shoulder they had been given at the scene of the accident. Billy had to be restrained by his brothers, but that hadn't stopped him from cursing his neighbors for not allowing them to assist in the rescue—technically, now, a recovery. Andrew and Earl followed their brother as he stomped away. Andrew took time to shake his fist at everyone while Cleve wondered who had notified the sheriff.

He had a pretty good idea.

"More likely you were returning to the scene of the crime," said the Spartanburg County deputy, laughing.

Andrew had reached for his beer. He pulled his hand back, the hand coming to rest on the pistol strapped to his belt. "What you mean by that?"

"It were an accident," said Billy, picking up a longneck.

"Uh-huh," said the deputy. "That's what they say."

Earl, whose red hair came by way of his mother's second husband, glanced at his half-brothers, then at Cleve sitting at the end of the table. "Well," Earl said to the deputy across the table from him, "that's what they told us. It were an accident."

Cleve crossed his leg and struck a match on the heel

of his boot. "What business is this of yours?" he asked the deputy.

"I'm a Laughlin and Laughlins are good haters."

Cleve snorted and busied himself with lighting his cigar.

Billy cleared his throat. He put down his beer. "What . . . what are they saying?"

Andrew glowered at the deputy. "Who cares? He's just trying to make trouble."

Instead of picking up his coke, Earl dry washed his hands under the table. How could this have happened? One moment he'd been drinking, the next he was involved in an accident that killed a whole family. How would he explain that to his wife?

The deputy sipped from his coke. "The last of the McKelveys goes off a bridge and our clan didn't have anything to do with it? Don't make sense." He glanced at the door leading to the main room. "People out there are watching to see what I'm going to do about it."

"What *are* you going to do?" inquired Cleve.

The deputy leaned back, opening his arms as he did. "Not my jurisdiction."

Someone shrieked at the card table and gathered in the pot.

Billy jumped, knocking over his longneck, and beer washed across the table before he was able to snatch it up. Earl scooted back and allowed the liquor to drip to the floor.

The woman sitting in the card player's lap got up and walked over. She snatched a rag off an empty chair, frowned at them, and wiped up the beer.

Once she returned to the card table, Andrew asked,

"Why you telling us this?"

The deputy shrugged. "Just thought you might want to take a trip through the Saluda Gap and stay in North Carolina until this calms down." The deputy studied Billy as he finished off his beer. "We don't need people making decisions when they're jumpy."

"Do I look jumpy?" asked Cleve, taking a drag off his cigar.

"You ain't telling me what to do," said Andrew. "Like Billy said, it were an accident."

"A most fortuitous accident for the Laughlin clan," said the deputy. "Most McKelveys live around Campobello, and Campobello *is* my jurisdiction. I'd watch my back while you're in Spartanburg County. A woman and her children died on that bridge."

"You threatening us?" Andrew returned his hand to the butt of his pistol.

The deputy glanced at the weapon. "You really want to throw down on me, Andrew? Today of all days, when the McKelveys, for all intents and purposes, are finished? Seems counterproductive."

"What?" Billy put down the beer he'd just finished off.

Andrew, Earl, and Cleve ignored the deputy. Using big words was the deputy's stock-in-trade since he'd moved to town. He was just showing off.

"I'm not going anywhere," said Earl. "I've got a farm to run." Earl had always been the most conscientious of the three.

Cleve watched Billy pick up Andrew's beer and down the remaining contents.

Andrew didn't seem to mind. "Just don't be

threatening us." He took his hand off the pistol.

"Yeah," said Billy, "it were an accident."

"You'd better have an alibi because sooner or later the Greenville County sheriff is going to come calling."

"He already has." Cleve blew cigar smoke across the table. "At the bridge."

"And what did you tell him, if I might be so bold as to ask?"

"Don't tell him nothing," Andrew warned Cleve. "I'm not afraid of any law. Besides, like the man said, we have an alibi."

"Yeah," said Billy, nodding. "We were drinking at Earl's." He glanced at the others.

The deputy noticed the untouched coke on the table in front of Earl. "You brew the stuff. I didn't think you drank it."

Earl didn't know what to say. He and Rebecca were working harder and harder for less and less, and these days, he found himself sneaking a sip or two to dull the pain.

Andrew laughed. "Earl was so drunk he couldn't get on his horse."

"Yeah," repeated Cleve, without any humor, "couldn't even get on his horse when it came time to go."

"Uh-huh." The deputy got to his feet. "Well, you boys enjoy your drinks; then you need to get back to Greenville County."

Andrew jutted out his jaw. "Like I asked: You telling us what to do?"

"Oh, no," said the deputy, smiling down before he walked away, "just a friendly recommendation." He glanced in the direction of the main room. "Didn't see any McKelveys out there so you're probably safe for the moment."

Andrew tried to follow him, but Cleve grabbed Andrew's arm and pulled him down in his chair.

"Calm down!" ordered his cousin.

Andrew shook off the hand. "I'll kill the sumbitch!" He glanced at his brothers. "And any McKelveys."

None of the poker players looked their way, only the brunette sitting in the lap of one of the players.

"Just the kind of talk we need," muttered Earl.

"Aw," complained Andrew, "don't be such a sissy."

"Speaking of girls," said Earl, getting to his feet, "Rebecca thinks I spend too much time with you boys."

"Well then," said Andrew, looking up at his brother, "get along to your quilting bee. I'm sure the other ladies are waiting for you down at the church."

This sparked an idea. To his half-brother, Earl said, "Billy, go see the preacher. You need to calm down."

Billy stopped finishing off Andrew's beer and looked up at him. "What you say?"

"Nah," said Cleve, shaking his head. "That's the last thing we need."

"That's right," said Andrew. "It'd get out."

"It'll get out sooner or later," said Earl.

"Then," said Cleve, "I prefer later."

"Nobody knows nothing," said Andrew, glancing around the table.

Billy gestured toward the ceiling with his bottle. "*He* knows."

"Oh, jiminy," muttered Andrew.

Cleve opened his jacket so Billy could see the pistol

strapped under his arm. "I know, too, and I'm the one you should worry about."

"Hey," said Earl, "watch how you talk now!"

Cleve looked up. "I don't mean shoot him now, and I don't mean with this gun. I'm pretty good with a rifle."

"You're nuts," said Billy, shaking his head. He called to the brunette at the poker table. "Hey, we could use a few more beers over here!"

The girl sighed, left the cardplayer's lap, and sashayed out the door.

Billy returned to his beer. After a few moments, he realized everyone was staring at him. "Aw, get along now. I ain't gonna talk, and especially to no preacher." But saying it didn't calm his nerves. Billy began rolling the bottle between his hands. "Still, somebody's got to make it right."

Cleve tapped his jacket. "You damned well better keep your mouth shut."

Everyone at the table knew Billy was a whiner, and none of them wanted to go to prison for some damned fool accident.

Cleve had to admit he didn't remember everything that had happened. One moment they were chasing the carriage, and the next, it vanished. Just disappeared.

Cleve had ridden onto the bridge to make sure the carriage was really gone. When he looked around, all he saw was Andrew taking Billy's reins—when Billy wanted to dismount—and they'd gotten the hell out of there.

What he did remember was drinking their way through a couple of jugs and complaining about the price of corn, not to mention the number of revenuers prowling around Glassy Mountain. The next thing Cleve knew, Earl was falling down drunk and everyone was laughing at him. When Cleve returned from taking a piss, he'd seen the McKelveys on the road below, a golden opportunity to fool with those people.

"I'm heading home, but who's got him." Earl motioned to Billy, whose head rested on his arms on the table.

"Get along then," said Andrew. "Cleve and I'll take care of him."

"Well, just don't beat him up too much."

"Right," said Cleve, grinning wickedly. "Just enough to miss Sunday services."

"We've got nothing to worry about," said Andrew. "Billy's family, and blood's thicker than water."

Billy raised his head, and they saw tears running down his cheeks. "It was an accident, I tell you . . . an accident."

The woman returned with the beers and tried not to stare. Was Billy Laughlin crying? When was the last time she'd seen a Laughlin cry?

Cleve threw some money on her tray. "Go on now. Get out of here."

Once she left, Earl said, "Keep him away from the preacher and we're probably okay. He just needs to think this through."

Cleve wasn't so sure. Sober, Billy wasn't that clear a thinker.

"Come on, Earl," said Andrew, taking a new beer. "Nobody turns on their brother."

"Uh-huh. What about Cain and Abel?"

Five

That same evening, James drove his wagon out of Greenville and in the direction of Anderson. Several miles down the road, he approached a thicket of trees and a bend in the track where the train slowed down. Off in the distance, perhaps ten or more miles away, a whistle sounded as the train approached a crossing.

That'll be our train, thought James. He slapped the reins across the rear of the horse and the animal increased its gait.

Hidden in the covered portion of the wagon, Allison McKelvey hunched over, waiting, watching. Tears ran down her cheeks. After wiping them away, she reproached herself. She should be more gay. James would not be pleased to have a crybaby on his hands.

Plainly, the girl was taken with this young man with the broad shoulders and ropey muscles. Not only had he rescued her from the river, but he had sat with her last night and talked in soothing tones, talked as her mother might have talked when she or one of her brothers suffered through an illness.

For most of the day, Allison had watched from the loft as James moved around the Belles' carriage house. His movements were so casual, and yet with a watchfulness that belied his easy manner, that she realized James lived with an expectation of trouble, never looking for it but always prepared. Her father had moved in a similar manner, and Allison had felt safe in his presence, just as she was feeling with James.

But could she tell him what was really on her mind? The train whistle meant she didn't have much time.

"James, those men should go to jail for what they did."

"Oh," said the young man, glancing over his shoulder into the interior of the wagon. "You're up. I wondered if I was going to have to wake you."

"I mean it. Those men should go to jail."

"And how would we do that?"

"Call the law."

"You want me to tell the law that I saw three, maybe four riders leaving the bridge, and you saw—"

"They killed my family!"

"You saw them do that? Those men on horseback?"

"We're McKelveys and they're Laughlins. Everybody knows our families have been feuding."

"And that's called supposition or conjecture. Did you actually see anything, Allison? Remember, it'd have to be something you could swear to on a Bible in a court of law. I thought you said your brothers pushed you down on the floorboard."

For a long time, Allison said nothing, then: "Well, they should pay."

"I agree, but sometimes you have to be a good coward before you can be a decent hero."

That wasn't how Allison took it. She was thinking that you had to understand how to use big words such as "supposition" and "conjecture," or nobody would pay you any mind.

"If I had a gun, I could make them pay. Sell me a gun, James. That's your business."

"Actions have consequences, Allison."

"And I want consequences for my family. It's in the Good Book. 'An eye for an eye.'"

James glanced over his shoulder. "You need to control that Scots–Irish temper of yours. Those old maids won't tolerate it."

"Then I'll go back to Glassy and settle accounts with the Laughlins myself."

James reined in his horse, then shifted around on the wooden seat and faced her.

When he only studied her, she said, "I know what's right."

"No. You and your people *think* you know what's right, then it's Katy bar the door 'cause there's no reasoning with you. What's going to happen in the next few hours will determine your life's course, a course that changed in a matter of seconds on that bridge. You can change your life tonight, and for the better, but one misstep, one mispoken word, and everything done for you by Margaret Belle can be wiped away in seconds."

The girl considered this. "It's not right," she finally said.

"Allison, my people are not your people. My people came to this country to have something to pass along to those who come along behind us. Your clan only wishes to pass along its pride and independence. That's why there're so many widows and orphans in the Dark Corner, and you want to take that pridefulness and independence into Belles Lodging, a place established to avoid violence. You'd better think twice, because the oldest of those three old maids, Helen Belle, will show you the door and you'll be out on the street once again."

He shook the reins and guided the horse and wagon toward the trees. Inside the tree line, James reined in the horse, stood up, and looked around, then leapt to the ground, taking along his rifle.

He sniffed the air. A doused campfire could be a dead giveaway for vagrants waiting to climb aboard when the train slowed to take the curve. Satisfied, James reached up and took Allison by the waist and helped her to the ground. Light as a feather, not the load he'd hauled out of the ravine last night.

Allison brushed down her dress and straightened her bonnet. This was the first time she'd ever been out after dark with a boy other than her brothers, and her sense of vulnerability quickly rid her of making anymore demands.

She wore a gray dress with a high waistline, much too large for her, and earlier in the day, Margaret Belle had returned to the carriage house and dyed her hair black. Belle women were known for their raven hair, pale skin, and blue eyes. The hair color was easy enough to come by. There was always plenty of black hair dye in a house full of old maids.

James tied off the animal, and stood, rifle in hand,

listening once again. Allison stood next to him holding a carpetbag, head jerking one way, then the other. She couldn't shake the vision of plunging off a bridge and falling . . . falling . . .

James saw this and took her arm. "Everything's going to be all right, Allison."

She tried to return his smile but failed.

James squeezed her arm, then released it and dug something out of his jeans. A shiny, thin thread hung from his hand, along with the cross.

Her mother's necklace! A poor, plain old thing, but it had been her mother's.

"Sorry. Almost forgot."

Allison took the necklace and gripped it in a fist. Again tears formed in her eyes. It took a moment to breathe.

She wiped away more tears. "Thank you."

"Something to remember her by, not something to remind you of what happened."

The whistle sounded way down the track.

"Time to go."

He took a copy of the *Piedmont* from under the seat and a dark-colored blanket he'd been sitting on, then motioned her to follow him up the grade.

Standing between the rails, neither one of them saw anyone up or down the track, only heard the train and saw its light. The headlamp's vertical shafts, as bright as the light penetrating straight ahead, warned pedestrians of the train's imminent approach.

James stuck the newspaper under his arm and helped her down the far side of the grade. "Here's where it gets tricky. You've got to throw your bag on the train and follow it aboard. You can't count on boxcars having an open door. Those bulls watch places like that. Go for a platform between cars. There might be a gate barring your way; if there is, let this one pass and we'll wait for another." He paused. "You're not afraid of the dark, I hope, 'cause I've got to return to the other side of the track or this won't work."

Allison gripped his arm as the train entered the bend a mile or so away. "You don't have to worry about me none. I've jumped on trains before, ridden one with my . . . with my brothers into Spartanburg, not that I had a carpetbag to throw aboard. I've never done that, but I'm good enough to knock mistletoe out of trees at Christmas."

James smiled down at her. She was a pretty thing with that new black hair of hers. "Where's mistletoe when you need it?"

Allison returned the smile as the train's headlamp illuminated them. "Somehow, I don't think mistletoe has ever kept you from taking what you wanted, Mr. Stuart."

Gosh, but this girl was bold.

James took her in his arms and kissed her. The girl didn't seem to mind and kissed him right back. The carpetbag dropped to the grade and James felt her hands at his waist. It felt good to hold her. Well, Margaret Belle, that's what comes of locking up a boy and girl all day and making them keep their hands to themselves.

James ended the kiss with a big hug. The whistle blew and the headlamp bathed them in light.

Allison grinned up at him. "Think I should miss this

one, and catch the next one?"

"Better not," said James, raising his voice over the sound. "I have a feeling Margaret Belle knows train schedules better than Sherlock Holmes." He handed her the blanket. "Don't forget this."

"And I won't forget your kindness. I'm just sorry you're not staying around."

He squeezed her hand. "Don't worry, Allison. Everything's going to be just fine. By the time the Belles finish with you, rich boys will come a-calling."

She arched an eyebrow. "What if I don't want to marry a rich man? What if I want to marry a man like you?"

"Oh, you don't want to marry a traveling man. They try a woman's patience." He gestured at the barbed-wire fence behind her. "Now, step over there and wrap this blanket around you. Turn away from the light, and you'll do just fine. Nobody'll be looking at this side of the track. You got that piece of cardboard?"

She tapped the carpetbag. "It's inside."

"Well, good luck to you, Miss McKelvey."

"Belle," she said with a warm smile. "I'm Catherine Belle now, and I appreciate everything you've done for me."

Allison took her bag and backed away. Down the other side of the grade, James snapped a match into a flame and lit the newspaper.

"And you, Mr. Stuart," she called, once she had the blanket wrapped around her, "make sure you come a-calling after you become a rich peddler. You might be real appealing by then."

Six

The train slowed as it approached the bend, and the engineer, fireman, conductor, and all those in the caboose stepped over to where they could examine the wooded area running a hundred or so yards alongside the track. This was a jumping-on place for hoboes, and James Stuart did not disappoint. Everyone onboard saw the man standing by the railroad tracks at a small fire.

On the other side of the track, Allison dropped the blanket and hurried up the grade where she grabbed a handle and swung aboard, bringing along the carpetbag. As chance would have it, her platform had not yet passed where James stood.

Allison smiled and waved, leaned out and waved some more. She'd really enjoyed their kiss and wondered when she'd see him again. Last night, his voice had been the only thing keeping her from another crying jag. But he probably knew that; otherwise, why would he have talked all evening without a single response from her?

James could quote from the Bible at will, along with telling stories such as "The Celebrated Frog of Calaveras County," and reciting poems, such as "I Hear America Singing." Allison figured America must be the United States of America, otherwise known as The Enemy in her family, though she never really understood why. After that, James related the story of Evangeline and Gabriel.

Allison fell in love with that poem—or perhaps, in the telling—then "The Legend of Sleepy Hollow," which could've been about the Dark Corner. James finished with "Fast Rode the Night . . . to save my lady." But when he tried to sing "Pack Up Your Troubles in Your Old Kit-Bag, and Smile, Smile, Smile," Allison sent a gale of laughter hurtling down from the loft. James Stuart couldn't sing a lick.

Staring at the girl sleeping on the crates when she returned to the carriage house, Margaret Belle had said, "We need to make plans for tomorrow night, and I'm afraid it'll be your job to learn just how tough this girl is."

James studied the slender form under the blanket. "I'll do what has to be done, Miss Belle. We have an orphanage in Charleston, and it's nothing more than a workhouse."

"That's not our decision to make. Either the girl joins our conspiracy or she'll be dead within a week. There's more than one Laughlin who comes to town Saturdays, and I wouldn't be surprised if those boys aren't feeling their oats about their murdering ways."

"I could take a rifle into the Dark Corner and put a bullet in several of them. I know all those back roads."

"Which would make you no better than them."

"But it'd make me feel a whole lot better. You didn't see her family after they took that tumble into the river."

Margaret intentionally changed the subject. "James, are those crates of weapons Allison is sleeping on?"

"I wasn't coming this way originally. I was supposed to have sold most of them before I reached Greenville."

A female voice carried through the ajar carriage house doors, calling for Margaret to return to the main house.

Margaret glanced at the girl again. "She's going to be a pretty thing when she grows up."

"If she gets the chance."

The conductor broke into Allison's thoughts as she stood between cars and watched the darkened landscape roll by. It was really something to be moving this fast. It wouldn't be anytime before they—

"Miss?" he asked, pushing open the door from one of the passenger cars.

When Allison turned around, she burst into tears. "Oh, sir, don't put me off again."

The conductor regarded her. "Miss, do you have a ticket?"

"I know I slipped aboard, but I can pay." Allison reached in her purse.

"I'm sorry, Miss, but why did you think I'd put you off?"

Tears ran down Allison's face, and she didn't have to fake them. "The last conductor put me off down in Anderson."

"And why would he do that?"

"It's the chickenpox, sir. My family all died of the pox, and I'm being sent to Richmond to live with my aunt."

The conductor stepped back. "Well, I'm glad to see you have the good sense to remain between cars."

Allison tried to hand him the money, but the conductor wouldn't take it.

She appeared to become strickened again. "Oh, sir, you're going to put me off, aren't you?"

"I'm afraid so. Next stop is Greenville, and I'll see you inside the depot, but from there you must make your own arrangements."

James watched the train disappear and wondered what Margaret Belle would think of him stealing a kiss from such a child. Probably call him a cradle robber.

How old had the girl told him she was?

Fourteen and him nineteen. Guess that did make him a cradle robber.

Last night, Margaret had returned to the carriage house with two plates of food, eating utensils, and two bottles of cola. She had not, evidently, told her sisters about the girl, only that Stuart would be sleeping with his wagon to ensure the contents' security.

"Under normal circumstances you'd not be left alone with this girl."

"Yes, ma'am," said James, getting to his feet from a bench just outside the double doors. "I understand."

"But if the neighbors can't see Allison, I can't see the harm."

James eyed the food. The one time he'd gone inside the carriage house, he hadn't seen the girl. So he'd taken a seat on a bench outside and waited for dinner. While he waited, the lady next door peered at him through her window. James ignored her and took to whittling. Soon afterwards, Margaret came out the back door of the lodging house with their food. One plate she gave to James, the other she took inside.

Not having eaten since breakfast, James gobbled his dinner and waited for the lodgers who would want to inspect his firearms. All would be turned away. The Belle sisters had a fierce hatred of weapons, and this was why James always arrived in Greenville at the end of his trip. It wasn't because of cotillion, but that did make a good excuse. This year, he'd miss that dance and be stuck out on the road, running his route in reverse. He didn't think it would be as profitable, and when he returned to Charleston, he'd be in trouble with his family.

The following morning, Margaret returned with breakfast and knocked on the carriage house doors. A few moments later, James stuck his head out.

While Dutton watched through her window, Margaret said, "My sisters believe you have guns in your wagon, James, and that's why you didn't ask to sleep inside last night."

Taking his plate and holding open one of the doors, he said, "You're welcome to look, Miss Belle."

Inside, Margaret approached the girl, who sat on the crates under the cover of the wagon, her face buried in her hands.

Margaret stood below her, the plate of food and cup of coffee in her hand. "Do you have any relatives with whom you can go live, young lady?"

The girl wiped her eyes and looked down. She shook her head.

"No one to take you in?"

Another shake of the head.

"We could place you with a good family—that's what the church would do. But would you be safe from the Laughlins?"

Allison stared at the plate of food and cup of coffee. She realized she was hungry.

"Did James explain my plan?" asked Margaret.

The girl nodded, scrambled to the edge of the crates, and sat there, dangling her legs off the rear of the wagon. When could she have that food?

"So you agree that this is the best course of action for you to have a chance at any future?"

More nodding from the girl, and staring at the food.

"Very well. I'll find some clothing, and tonight James will smuggle you out of town. Today, while he's making his calls, you're not to go outside. The hired man may be in and out. His name is Eugene, but you're not to speak to him, nor are you to let on that you're in here. This is critical for making my plan work."

Margaret looked around. At one time the family carriage had been sheltered in here. Now, that side of the building was occupied by a Buick touring car driven by an employee of Woodside Mills in the last Main Street Hill Climb. The Buick had come in third.

"I'll bring out a pitcher of water, a towel, and a

chamber pot. Make use of them all. And take a nap. I have several things to teach you before you leave tonight and you need to be rested."

She handed the food and coffee to the girl. "Hide in the loft, Allison. It worked for me when I was your age."

Again the girl nodded, and this time she smiled.

Margaret stared at the crates, smelled the oil, and wondered if the rifles sold by James Stuart had been the ones responsible for the death of this girl's family.

Probably so, but with the war only a generation or so removed, no one had the nerve to tell anyone they couldn't own any weapons. Who knew when Yankees would return?

There was talk of war in Europe and the building of another camp outside Greenville. During the Spanish-American War, Camp Wetherill had been a boon to the local economy, and the city fathers wouldn't rest until another bunch of Federals strutted around town again, spending their greenbacks and acting like they owned the place.

Seven

"You had no right doing this!"

Helen stopped her pacing and took a drag off her cigarette. She was a thin woman with a narrow face and gray hair pulled back into a tight bun; the only sister to wear glasses. At this hour of the evening she wore a housecoat over her nightgown, the belt pulled tight revealing her thinness. Expelling a smoke-filled breath, the oldest of the three Belle sisters glared at Margaret, who sat at the dressing table with her back to her, brushing her hair the nightly one hundred strokes.

"We vote on such matters."

"I had to make a decision, and I made it." Margaret pulled the brush through her wondrously coal-black hair. Not a strand of gray, and about this Margaret was quite proud. "Besides, you and Mary Kate were at the church bazaar all day."

"More likely you waited for us to leave for church so you could finagle this situation, and now we're stuck with this girl."

"Oh, I don't know," said Mary Kate from where she lazed on the four-poster bed and pulled the ribbon on yet another Hershey's kiss. Chocolate was Mary Kate's passion, and since she had discovered the kisses, the chocolate had added more than a few pounds to her hips. "You can always turn out the girl."

"Oh, why such half measures?" asked Margaret, speaking to the mirror. "Just take her to the end of Court Street and drop her off. We all know what happens to young girls who lose the protection of their families."

"Well," said Mary Kate, smiling from the bed, "at least those who don't have an older sister to watch over them." Mary Kate's cherubic face belied a quick wit. She popped the kiss into her mouth. Her hair was already in rag rollers.

"Just whose side are you on, Mary Kate?" Helen pushed her glasses back on her nose. She needed to put her hair in rollers, too, but business first, such as the survival of Belles Lodging.

Mary Kate licked the chocolate from her fingers. "I'm on the side of any orphan."

"You'd take in all orphans?"

"Not at all. Just the ones threatened by soldiers."

The mention of which was enough to return the women to just such a day.

The Yankees had arrived at their plantation, looted the place, and dispersed the servants. Margaret, only ten years old, didn't emerge from her hidey-hole for two days. During this raid, Mary Kate, the former Sweetheart of Laurens County, discovered how much she'd missed young men during the war, and Helen learned not to talk back to Yankees. She bore the sergeant's mark for close to a week.

In the years following the war, the sisters—having moved to Greenville—convened nightly on the second floor to discuss the affairs of Belles Lodging. But as the women became more set in their ways, and the conversations became more heated—especially when it came to economies—the sisters no longer sat cross-legged on the four-poster bed, backs against the posts, hair in rollers. Nowadays one of them might lounge on the bed, as Mary Kate was doing, another sit on the chair from the dressing table, or perhaps lie across the chaise lounge where Margaret slept.

Never far from their minds was the loss of their plantation home when carpetbaggers had discovered the property on the delinquent tax roll. Only by selling the family silver, retrieved from the well where it had been thrown when the Yankees passed through, was it possible to hold onto the Greenville town house where brother John and his wife, Theresa, lived.

A three-story structure with steep gables, pointed windows, and a wrapound porch, the Belles' fifteen-room home had enough bedrooms to take in lodgers, especially when brother John decamped to the attic, his wife's complaints still ringing in his ears about how ugly he'd become, so disfigured and crippled from the war that she absolutely refused to be seen with him in public.

Theresa moved in with her mother in Spartanburg and she had been seen in the company of scalawags who wished to marry her for Belles Lodging; that is, if that fine home on West Washington Street could ever be sold.

John wouldn't give his wife the time of day, much less a divorce, so after a judge declared him of sound mind, Theresa's new friends had little use for her. She continued living with her mother, and whenever Theresa took a notion to return to Greenville, her sister-in-law met her at the door.

"You live here," said Helen, "and not only will you pull your share of the load, you'll sleep in my brother's bed."

"But, Helen, it gets hot up in that attic."

"Sorry, but that's the way it'll be. We don't have a single unoccupied room."

For this reason, Theresa never spent another night at Belles Lodging, and John never came downstairs. When plumbing was added to the house, including a bathroom for the second floor, a bath was added at the rear of the attic for brother John.

The first two levels of the house held six rooms each, and to economize, the sisters slept in the master bedroom on the second floor, the older two in the four-poster bed; Margaret relegated to a chaise lounge, one of those with a gently rising headboard, the same piece of furniture she'd slept on as a child.

Below the master bedroom lay the parlor with an arc at one corner, and in this semicircle sat an upright piano; at the attic level the semicircle became a turret where brother John sat in a rocking chair and watched Greenville grow and change; in the master bedroom, the half-circle held the four-poster bed.

Arranged around the walls of the bedroom were three armoires, a secretary where Helen kept the ledger, and next to the secretary, an old steamer trunk. Shelved next to the Belle family Bible was the *Book of Common Prayer, Women and Economics,* and the poems of Emily Dickinson. Also on this shelf lay a stack of *Forerunner* magazines, serializing *Herland,* a story about three male explorers who discover an all-female society, a society appearing to be superior to their own male-dominated one. Written by a leading feminist of the day, the discovery forces the explorers to reexamine their assumptions about the roles of women in a male-dominated world.

Still, with the potential seizure of their home by John's wife, the three sisters bit their tongues when men at the dinner table commented about secretaries and women working in retail shops along Main Street.

"They can only become coarsened by such experiences," said one traveling salesman.

"The building of the cigar factory near the Reedy River Falls is a sure sign of such decadence," said another. "It's one thing to strengthen the local economy by bringing in farmers' daughters to work in a mill, quite another for your own sisters to be tempted to abandon hearth and home."

"I've been told two hundred girls and young women are employed rolling cigars," said Robert Patton. "Their employers justify such hiring by citing the dexterity of the feminine hand."

The salesman cleared his throat before saying, "Those hands should be changing diapers and preparing meals for husbands returning home after a long day's work."

By holding their tongues, the Belles had survived the

war, Reconstruction, and several financial panics, but most importantly, they had kept their home out of the hands of their grasping sister-in-law. Nevertheless, the thought of a fourteen-year-old girl coming to live with them sent tremors through their tightly knit society. It was one thing to sit around and plan an uprising against a male-dominated society, but a loose-tongued child might bring an extra load of misery to the Old Maids' Club.

Margaret pulled the brush through her hair and looked at her sisters in the mirror. "We're all familiar with the feuds raging in the foothills, and I, for one, will not sit by and watch as one of these feuds claims yet another victim."

Helen sneered at her reflection. "How are you to prevent *our* lives from becoming entangled when the Laughlins come looking for the person who can put a noose around their collective necks?"

Margaret put down her brush and faced them. "I'm glad you asked, because I have a plan."

Eight

Evidently the plan was for everyone to be woken up in the middle of the night, and though the sisters had been apprised of Margaret's plan, Helen and Mary Kate were still struggling into their housecoats when Margaret left the chaise lounge at the sound of the front doorbell.

Margaret snapped on the upstairs hall light, and lodgers stuck their heads out of their rooms demanding to know if the house was on fire. The traveling salesmen who took rooms at Belles Lodging were prepared for such an eventuality, as the last things they hauled into their rooms at night were an axe and a length of rope. Nothing could be worse than being trapped in an inferno, and that's what these old wooden structures became when a fire broke out.

Margaret flew down the stairs and flipped on the front-porch light. At the same time, the grandfather clock bonged three-thirty. Eugene, the hired man, who slept in the basement, sharing a room with the coal bin and the canning from the previous summer, thumped upstairs, pushed open the basement door, and asked if he should call the fire brigade. Robert Patton, who rented one of the ground-floor rooms, was already heading to the front door in his nightshirt, stocking cap, and slippers.

"No, no, Robert," shouted Margaret. "I have it! I have it!"

Hoping her face was not too flushed, Margaret paused to catch her breath. When she patted down her hair she realized it was in rag curlers, and this induced another bout of flushing. Telling herself to calm down, she pulled open the door and found a policeman on the wraparound porch.

The officer removed his hat. "Sorry to disturb you at this hour, Miss Belle, but I thought it best I bring you the news. Nothing you'd want people yakking about on the party line."

He reached behind him and ushered Allison around to stand beside him. Allison smiled nervously. Tied around her neck was a piece of string, and attached to the string, a piece of cardboard. The feminine scrawl on the cardboard read: *I am Catherine Belle of New Orleans, Louisiana. Please deliver me to the Belle Sisters on West Washington Street in Greenville, South Carolina. They will pay all expenses.* In one hand the girl held a purse, in the other a carpetbag.

Oh, no! thought Margaret. Anyone who knows my handwriting will recognize it! That also went for the envelope the girl produced from her purse.

Allison performed a modified curtsy, as she had been taught yesterday in the carriage house. "Miss Belle,

I'm Catherine Belle from New Orleans, Louisiana, and you're my aunt."

Being flustered at their first encounter turned out to be easier than she'd imagined. Margaret took the envelope, tore it open, and stared at the page, taking a moment to gather her thoughts.

Her handwriting again! Why hadn't she thought of that?

"Catherine arrived less than an hour ago," continued the policeman, "and when the stationmaster called, I went down and walked her over."

"I . . . I wonder why the stationmaster didn't call us?" was all Margaret could think to ask.

"Well, Miss Belle," said the policeman, "we can't have you ladies wandering the streets in the middle of the night, can we? Might give the wrong impression."

"Of course," she said rather stiffly.

He gestured at the letter. "Does her story sound right? There's no way to check with the telephone lines down. Catherine mentioned something about her family drowning in that hurricane that struck New Orleans a few weeks back. You know, when it poured here. The church auxilary paid for her ticket to Greenville, but Catherine says she's lost it."

Allison clutched her purse and the handle of the carpetbag. She stared at her feet. Boarders from the ground-floor rooms gathered at the front door, as did the other two sisters, finally descending from upstairs.

"I'm sorry we meet under such circumstances. By all means, Catherine, do come in."

When Margaret gestured with the letter toward the interior of the house, Helen snatched the sheet of paper from her hand.

"Hmm," said the older sister, examining the scrawl through her glasses. "I do believe I recognize this handwriting."

Margaret tried to grab the letter, but Helen stepped back, tripping over Robert Patton. The middle-aged man caught the older woman, saving Helen from a fall, and for his trouble received a severe look. By then, Allison stood in the hallway, the policeman was heading down the front steps, and Mary Kate was closing the door.

"Sorry for the disturbance," said Mary Kate, smiling all around. "Please return to your rooms." She pulled her robe tight and touched at the rollers in her hair.

Margaret took Allison's bag. "I'm sure you've had a long and tiring trip, my dear. Why don't you come upstairs?"

She escorted the girl across the foyer and up the stairs where the curious huddled at the second-floor landing: several traveling salesmen and Victoria Lee and her daughter, Betty Jean. Lee and her daughter wore the most fashionable robes, though they were practically penniless.

Coming upstairs behind them, Helen repeated, "Like I said, I know this handwriting."

Margaret put her head down and continued to trudge upstairs.

"This girl's not our niece, Margaret."

Allison turned around, causing Helen to pause on the stairs below. Robert Patton had been shuffling toward his room, but upon hearing this, he wandered over to the bottom of the stairs and looked up.

"You're right," said Allison. "I'm not your niece."

Helen smiled and the lodgers leaned close, especially

the girl, Betty Jean. She peered through the balusters at this new arrival.

"I'm your second cousin, twice removed," said Allison, "but 'Aunt Margaret' has a nicer ring to it."

From below them on the stairs, Mary Kate laughed. "Yes, it does, doesn't it?"

"Character," preached Helen as she shook her cigarette in the face of Allison, who sat in the chair belonging to the dressing table. "Everything begins with character, young lady, and none of us knows your character, but we do know you're clever."

"What Helen means—"

"I know what she means, Aunt Margaret. And I'm a good girl. You don't have to worry about me none."

"You don't have to worry about me," said Mary Kate from the bed, where she pulled the tab on another Hershey's kiss. "The 'none' is unnecessary."

Allison nodded to the woman on the bed. "You don't have to worry about me," she repeated.

"Correct." Mary Kate peeled the foil from the chocolate kiss. "You're not in Kansas anymore."

Helen turned on her sister. "Pardon?"

"It's from *The Wonderful Wizard of Oz.* Really, Helen, you should get your nose out of all that Sigmund Freud. Everyone knows the man's nuts."

"I'm trying to have a serious conversation here, Mary Kate."

"That would be: I'm trying to have a serious conversation. Only Southerners are excessively concerned with place." She winked at Allison.

Allison looked at Margaret, confused.

The youngest of the three old maids smiled warmly from the chaise lounge. "Nothing to worry about, my dear. Just the usual family bickering."

"This is no joke." Helen gestured at Allison with her cigarette. "We only have your word, don't we, that you're a young woman of good character." After Helen took a drag from her cigarette, she stood there, leaning back, arm across her chest, and regarded the girl through her glasses.

"My word's good." Allison glanced at the other two sisters. "Us McKelveys don't lie."

"We McKelveys don't lie," said Mary Kate, "or simply 'McKelveys don't lie.'"

Allison turned to Margaret. "But you said I was to never use that name again."

Mary Kate laughed. "Seems like the girl's a better confidence man than you are, Helen."

Her sister let out another smoke-filled breath and pushed her glasses up. "And that's just what she may be: a grifter."

Though the bedroom was exceptionally large, Allison felt the walls closing in and her face about to explode. It did. She burst into tears, burying her face in her hands. It was simply too much: her family dead, hiding all day in the carriage house, and now she had to be perfect for these old ladies.

Mary Kate and Margaret left their seats, huddled around her, and patted her shoulders. "There, there, my dear," said the two women.

Allison peered through her fingers, measuring the distance between the chair where she sat and the bedroom door.

She couldn't do this. No, no, not without help from her mama or her daddy. Or James Stuart. James had pulled her out of the river and hidden her from the Laughlins, but now there were only these old women, and they expected too much, not to mention they spoke a language she understood but couldn't speak, at least not to their standards.

"See what you've done, Helen."

"You're being especially cruel."

The older sister was unmoved. She took another drag off her cigarette and the smoke came racing from her nose. "The tears mean only that she's weak and undependable."

"Oh, don't be so mean!"

"That is so disgusting."

Allison snuffled into her hands. Mary Kate furnished a handkerchief. Allison used it to wipe her eyes.

"Dab at your eyes," said Mary Kate. "A lady doesn't wipe away her tears, but dabs at them, and sometimes she takes a considerable amount of time doing so."

Allison stared at the woman. Couldn't she do anything right?

The two sisters returned to stroking Allison while Helen walked over to the secretary and stubbed out her cigarette in an ashtray on the drop-down desk.

"You two seem to have forgotten that we were once in the same predicament. We had to toughen up . . . so does this girl."

Allison heard this, but it made no sense. How could women who lived in such a splendid home know any pain or sorrow? Why, they even had electricity!

Allison blew her nose and wiped it. From the corner of her eye, she saw Mary Kate shaking her head.

Now what? Ladies don't blow their noses? Allison straightened up. Well, she wasn't a lady, she hadn't lived in a city, and she sure didn't want to live here now!

Mary Kate was explaining that Allison didn't have to go through what they'd had to endure.

Wiping her hands on her housecoat, her older sister said, "I have no idea how fair play has anything to do with this."

More protesting from the other sisters until Allison cleared her throat. "I know who my parents are and I miss them, that's all."

Helen shrugged. "I know who my parents were and I miss them, too, Allison."

"Helen," said Margaret, practically tapping her foot, "that's much too harsh. You were nineteen years old when our parents died. I was ten. I know how this child feels."

The older sister glanced at the bedside alarm clock. "Well, we're to be up in an hour. Boarders depend on us, but I imagine you two think that's unfair, too, after being up so late."

"Where will she sleep?" This from Mary Kate.

"Ask Margaret," said Helen, heading for the four-poster bed. "I'm sure the sleeping arrangements are part of her master plan."

Margaret pulled Allison from the chair and tugged her toward the bedroom door. "Come along, Catherine. I'm sure it's been a while since you've had a decent meal. I'll fix some breakfast."

Helen stretched and yawned. "Just don't make any noise coming back to bed."

"You're going back to bed?" asked Mary Kate, following Margaret and Allison to the door.

Helen had been untying her robe. She glanced at the alarm again. "Allison, you do know how to cook, don't you?"

"Yes, ma'am. Ma was teaching me . . . ."

She bent over at the waist and gagged. Tears ran down her cheeks. She couldn't do this, she just couldn't.

Margaret put an arm around the girl and gave her a sideways hug. "Everything's going to be all right, Catherine."

"Surely a comfort," said Helen, pulling tight the sash on her robe, "but hardly relevant."

Breathing heavily, Allison straightened up and tried again. "I can bake bread, fry chicken, boil corn—"

"But can you cook gumbo?" asked the eldest sister.

"What's gumbo?"

Helen chuckled. "And this child is supposed to be from New Orleans? What *were* you thinking, Margaret?"

"I was thinking that because of the hurricane, the lines are down between here and New Orleans and it might be several weeks before anyone could learn the fate of Catherine's family."

"But we don't have several weeks to turn this girl into a Belle, only an hour or so before the lodgers start peppering her with questions."

Nine

When the four women entered the kitchen, a large room behind the main house, they passed through a short hallway flanked by two pantries. There were no doors on either pantry, so Allison got a quick look at rows of paper and cloth sacks, cardboard boxes, and large cans of food. Both the kitchen and the pantries illustrated the orderliness with which the sisters ran Belles Lodging. After all, each of them had almost fifty years' experience at squeezing the dollar until the eagle squawked.

Helen flicked on the ceiling light and picked up some kindling lying on top of several wedges of seasoned wood stacked in a firewood rack. She opened the mouth of a cast-iron stove and tossed in the small bundle, followed by several pieces of seasoned wood, then a match. The fire would burn for the rest of the day, sometimes intensely, sometimes just enough to keep food warm.

To Allison the kitchen was an amazing place, a huge room with pots and pans hanging from the walls and a long table in the middle. Two sinks sat beside each other and a stack of drying cloths sat on a counter nearby. Over the sinks was a lone window, with ruffled curtains tied back; through the darkened glass Allison saw the dim outline of the carriage house. In the distance streetlights glowed. A ticking clock occupied the only remaining wallspace.

Cabinets and open shelves covered the walls, many cabinets missing their doors. Shelves were filled with dishes and glassware. Cups hung on hooks under the cabinets, and to Allison it appeared the Belles could feed a small army. Rows of silverware lay on one counter along with stacks of cloth napkins. Farthest from the stove stood a large metal box.

"What's that?" asked Allison.

Helen glanced at the machine. "Refrigerator."

"What's a refrigerator?"

"An icebox cooled by electricity," explained Margaret. "No more emptying water pans or waiting for the next ice delivery."

This made absolutely no sense to Allison. When electricity worked properly, it was a marvelous invention turning night into day. Allison had seen that in Greer, but she'd also seen electricity spark and burn when it didn't work properly. It made no sense for something so hot to make anything so cold.

"You probably had a refrigerator in New Orleans," said Helen, "where you were born and raised. The motor and compressor are outside or the smell of ammonia would drive us from the room." She looked at her sister. "Catherine was born and raised in Louisiana, wasn't she?"

Margaret didn't know.

"Go ahead, Allison," said Mary Kate. "Open the door and look inside."

Allison didn't move.

"Just pull the handle," encouraged Mary Kate. "It's like your icebox at home."

"I thought we weren't to make any references to her past or call her by her former name," said Helen, fitting an apron over her robe. Usually, the sisters wore cotton skirts and long-sleeved shirtwaists, ordinary patterns drawn from *The Modern Priscilla.*

"You're the one who mentioned New Orleans."

"Yes, but New Orleans is where she lived, right, Catherine?"

Happy to be off the hook about the electric icebox, Allison said, "Yes, ma'am. I was born and raised in New Orleans, Louisiana."

"Well," said Mary Kate, turning to a shelf filled with cookbooks, "the Belles of New Orleans had money, and it's hot as Hades down there, so I'd imagine—"

"Mary Kate!" cautioned Margaret. "Watch your language."

"Oops! Sorry, Catherine."

"Don't worry, ma'am. I've heard worse."

"Well," said Helen, taking down a can marked Maxwell House Hotel, Nashville, Tenn., "you won't hear that language in this house. Any lodger who's profane or vulgar will be shown the door. We have a reputation to maintain."

"Visitors," explained Margaret, "and especially widows and their children, know they can reside at Belles and their ears won't be assaulted by words and phrases heard on the street."

"I thought there were laws against bad language."

"If a woman's husband presses the issue, such laws would be enforced, but how would a widow enforce such a law?"

"Another reason women should have the vote," said Helen, spooning ground coffee into a measuring cup.

Margaret continued. "A woman can't complain to the courts. Not only does she have no standing, but she might have to utter such words on the record, and that would mean, by definition, that she was no lady."

"Pardon me," said Helen, pouring the ground coffee from the measuring cup into a glass container shaped like an hourglass, "but how is this helping Catherine become oriented to Greenville?"

Mary Kate, who had been searching for the *Fannie Farmer,* found the worn, dog-eared book practically in pieces. "I wonder if there's a recipe for gumbo."

Helen snorted. Breakfast was eggs and grits, sausage or bacon, biscuits and homemade jams, not gumbo. She poured water from the sink faucet into the hourglass-shaped glass container. It looked like no coffeepot Allison had ever seen.

Helen saw the girl's look. "Ask your questions, child."

"What . . . what's that?"

Helen cut her eyes at Mary Kate, who thumbed through the *Fannie Farmer.* "Our latest extravagance. Mary Kate insisted on it. It's a Silex coffeemaker."

Running her finger down the table of contents, Mary Kate said, "But it makes the best cup of coffee."

"A complete waste of money," said Helen. "Do you drink coffee, Catherine?"

"Yes, ma'am, I do."

Margaret nudged Allison onto one of the long-legged stools on the far side of the preparation table. "Only makes one cup at a time. Not what we use for boarders." Margaret smiled. "So this first cup will be for you—our new niece."

Mary Kate squealed. "Oh, look! Gumbo!"

Helen shook her head wearily.

Margaret took a seat on a stool beside Allison. "Helen's right. We need to know more about you. It's not enough to know you arrived last night—I mean this morning—from New Orleans and your family died in the storm. There must be more, and we all must agree on the same story."

"But . . . but that's all I know, Miss Margaret. That's all you told me."

"Aunt Margaret," corrected Mary Kate, turning pages in the cookbook. "Listen here." She read the recipe for gumbo.

"Andouille sausage?" asked Helen. "Not only what is that, but where do you find it?"

"Hmm, I've read about this before. It's some kind of hot sausage." Mary Kate shook her head. "No, no, it says the sausage is optional." She paused. "That doesn't make any sense."

"We might get the sausage from Ballentines', but the shrimp, where in the world are we going to get shrimp? We don't live anywhere near the coast."

"I wonder if that new place, Pearce-Young-Angel, carries shrimp. They're doing some amazing things with refrigerated railroad cars." Mary Kate chewed on her lip. "Maybe someone at the Court Street curb market has heard of andouille sausage."

"Oh, forget the gumbo," said Margaret. "The girl needs to know about her family. And that would be in the family Bible." Margaret left the kitchen, disappearing through the hallway leading to the front of the house.

Allison slipped off the stool, almost following her. All the joy she'd felt at being alive . . . replaced by the despair of losing her family. Tears again ran down her cheeks, and she returned to the stool, shoulders slumping.

"There, there," said Mary Kate, walking around to pat the girl on the shoulder again. "Don't worry, Catherine. We'll figure out how to make gumbo."

Allison buried her face in her hands and sobbed.

"You must buck up, girl," said Helen, heading for the refrigerator. "You hear me?"

Allison had never felt such despair. She'd never see her family again. Never play with her brothers. Wiping away her tears, Allison sat up. "I need to attend their funeral."

"What?" asked Mary Kate, placing a metal bowl on the counter.

"Whose funeral?" asked Helen, retrieving a hunk of bacon from one of the refrigerators and closing the door with her bottom.

Allison found she had more tears to wipe away. Sometimes these crying jags simply overwhelmed her. "My family's."

"Well, that's quite imposs . . . ."

Helen's voice drifted off as a middle-aged man came through the kitchen door. He wore a flannel shirt, overalls, and a pair of old military boots.

"Funeral?" He looked from Allison to the two sisters and back to the girl again. "What'd I miss? Who died?"

Ten

"The girl's overwrought," said Helen, placing the chunk of bacon on the preparation table. "She's . . . she's . . . ."

Mary Kate put down the flour tin. "She's just realized she's safe."

"Safe in the bosom of her family," added Helen. Goodness gracious but they did not need these questions, and Helen had a premonition such questions would never end. Still, she would do her duty by this orphan. Her sisters would remind her of that.

Mary Kate gave Allison another hug. "There, there, Catherine, everything's going to be all right. We'll buy some new clothes and you'll feel right at home."

Margaret came through the door with a large Bible in her hands. "Catherine's mother was Jeanne and your father's name—"

"Eugene!" cried out Mary Kate from where she stood on the other side of the table.

Margaret looked up from the Bible. "Oh, I didn't know

you were up." She closed the book with an audible thump.

"I'm always up by five." The hired man looked at Helen. "You can always depend on that newfangled alarm clock your sister got me. I didn't bring no rooster from Greenwood."

"But, Eugene," said Mary Kate, fumbling for something to say, "winter's coming on and you know how the boarders complain about the cold."

Looking at Helen again, Eugene said, "I know how some people complain."

Eugene and his wife were from Greenwood County, but they did not live together. Florie lived in a tent at the Hopewell Tuberculosis Association out on Rutherford Road, a pioneer tuberculosis camp established by Mrs. Harry Haynsworth and Mrs. Mary Gridley. Twice a week, Eugene took food from the Belles' kitchen to Hopewell and shared it with the patients.

He sniffed the air. "Is that coffee?"

"Brewed the first cup for you," said Helen, cutting her eyes at Allison.

"Don't mind if I do."

Margaret, holding the Bible behind her back, explained to Allison who Eugene was and where he slept.

"At no charge," finished Helen.

"It's like sleeping in a coal bin. Surprised I don't have TB myself." Eugene took a cup from a hook under an open cupboard. "Nice to meet you, Catherine. I'm sure you'll enjoy being here, no matter where they bunk you."

Helen poured coffee from the Silex coffeemaker into his cup.

After taking a sip, Eugene looked over the lip at Margaret. "You were looking up Catherine's family . . . why?"

"Well . . ."

Mary Kate returned from the pantry with a can of lard. "She wanted to update the information about Catherine's family."

"Update dead people?" Eugene frowned. "What's the use?"

"For the family." Mary Kate started with a can opener on the lard can. "You know, when we pass on."

Eugene shivered. He'd buried his share of soldiers during the Spanish-American War, and most of those soldiers had died from yellow fever, not any Spaniard's bullet. He took another sip of coffee to alleviate the sudden chill.

Helen pulled on a pair of heavy gloves lying on top of the seasoned wood in the firewood rack and placed a couple of additional wedges in the stove. "You fill the hopper?" she asked.

Belles Lodging had been converted to central heating, but someone had to fill the coal hopper twice a day. Located in the basement, the hopper fed the furnace. The resultant heat was distributed by water circulating through pipes to radiators in every room of the house but the kitchen and the new bathrooms.

"I was going to finish this here coffee first."

"Well," said Helen, slamming shut the stove door and removing the gloves, "let me know when to start your breakfast." She tossed the gloves on the stack of wood.

"It'll take the same amount of time it usually takes."

Eugene sipped again from his cup and returned to the basement.

"You know," said Mary Kate, dumping some measured flour into a metal bowl, "Catherine's been here only a couple of hours and my nerves are already frayed."

"I'm . . . I'm sorry," stammered Allison.

"Don't take that personally," said Margaret. "Mary Kate occasionally has attacks of the vapors."

"Probably needs another of those chocolate kisses," said Helen, taking a large knife from a drawer. "That usually does the trick." She reached for a platter on one of the shelves, took it down, and placed the platter in the center of the table.

"Is there . . . is there anything I can do?"

"No, my dear," said Margaret, patting her hand, "you just sit there and get used to being here. This is your home now."

Helen gave the bacon an eyeball measurement, marked the spot with the knife, and started slicing.

Soon Allison was sniffling again. She thought she'd cried herself out with all the time she'd spent in the carriage house, that there couldn't be more tears, but here they came again, running down her face, choking off her breath.

"Catherine," said Helen, without looking up from slicing bacon, "the time for tears is over."

"Unless you need them to get out of a difficult situation," contributed Margaret.

"Difficult situation?" Allison stopped with a little choking breath. She wiped away the tears. "I . . . I don't understand. I cry when I get hurt." Thinking of her family, she added, "Or when somebody hurts me."

Mary Kate brushed her hands together and the flour flew. "My, my, but this girl has a lot to learn."

"You know," said Helen, finally looking up from the chunk of bacon and pushing her glasses up on her nose, "something's going to have to be done about Catherine's accent. She sounds a bit too nasal for my taste."

Margaret saw the look of alarm on the girl's face. "Don't worry, my dear. You'll learn to drop your voice into your chest." To her sisters, Margaret said, "Maybe Catherine was raised outside New Orleans like other French Huguenots. Cooper Hill, the ancestral home of the Belles, is outside Charleston."

"I've told you more than once," said Mary Kate, heading around the table and for the refrigerator, "French Huguenot is redundant. Huguenots *are* French."

"I'm Scots-Irish," said Allison.

Helen looked up from the bacon. "I hadn't thought of it, but are you related to the outlaw Allison McKelvey?"

The girl nodded. "I was named for him."

From the refrigerator where she took a bottle of buttermilk, Mary Kate straightened up. "We were so fixated on the Belle family, we never noticed."

Margaret laughed. "Nor considered the fact that the Allison McKelvey we know of was a man."

"He wasn't really an outlaw," said Allison. "That's what Banastre Tarleton called him, 'cause he couldn't catch him."

"I'll bet your ancestor was acquainted with ours." Mary Kate returned to the bowl and splashed in some buttermilk. "We're related to John and Alicia Belle. John fought at Cowpens and Kings Mountain, and his wife stood down Christian Huck, who wanted to burn their home in Spartan District."

Though she might be poorly educated, Allison was Southern enough to feel right at home discussing ancestors. "They say Allison was killed at Guilford Courthouse, but they never found the body."

"Always good for a legend." Helen picked up an iron skillet and placed it on the stove.

Margaret opened the Bible and pointed at the top of the inside cover. "We're all descendants of Catherine Belle. Catherine and Nelie Belle arrived in Charleston in 1718. John was Catherine's youngest child. Family legend holds that Nelie was kidnapped by Blackbeard the Pirate and rescued by a pirate hunter by the name of . . ."

The sisters stared at Allison, their mouths hanging open.

"James Stuart," finished Mary Kate.

Helen shook her head. "Bunch of nonsense, if you ask me."

Mary Kate returned to her biscuit mix. After giving the bowl several stirs with a wooden spoon, she poured in more buttermilk. "John Belle, our great-grandfather, sailed to England to bring his brother back from studying law."

"He wasn't studying," commented Helen. "He was a rake."

Margaret glanced at Allison. "Should we be talking about this in front of Catherine? I don't mean family secrets, but the language is rather crude."

Mary Kate added more buttermilk and picked up the spoon again. "I daresay Allison knows what a rake is."

The girl's blank look told them all they needed to know.

"A libertine," explained Helen.

Another blank look.

Mary Kate returned to stirring her batter. "I can see we have our work cut out for us."

"Well," said Margaret, "no one ever accused those living in the Dark Corner of being too worldly."

"Pa said that's why we lived there," said Allison, "to keep the city at bay."

The sisters stared at her again.

"I'm sorry if that was impolite."

"Oh, you weren't being impolite," said Margaret, chuckling. "You've given us a lesson in humility. Greenvillians may know a thing or two, but only because we live in another world. People from the Dark Corner simply understand a different world."

Now it was Allison's turn to stare. Why didn't these ladies know that? They were supposed to be really smart people.

Mary Kate laid a cloth on her end of the preparation table and spread it out. She used a sifter to shake out flour. "So, do I finish my story or not?" She dumped the gooey contents of the bowl onto the floured cloth.

Helen sighed. "Go ahead."

"On the return voyage from England, John Belle met our great-grandmother, Alicia Bentley. They later married and moved to Spartan District. Probably the only Huguenots in this part of the state."

"Well, there's the Lanneau family," corrected Helen. "One ran the Huguenot Mill until it closed in '07."

"Your people were Presbyterians, weren't they?" Margaret asked of Allison.

The girl looked at the table. "Yes," she said softly.

"We're Episcopalians."

Mary Kate took out the rolling pin. "Probably not a significant difference."

"But if she wants to attend the Presbyterian Church," said Margaret, "that'll be fine with us."

"Pardon? She must attend our church," said Mary Kate, applying the rolling pin to the biscuit mix. "I've never heard of family members attending different churches. That's what church is all about—family."

"Which reminds me," said Helen, moving the platter near the stove, "anyone remember what day of the week it is?"

Margaret, Mary Kate, and Allison looked at her, then at the clock.

"Sunday!"

"Church!"

Mary Kate clapped her hands and the flour flew. "Oh, goody, she'll get to see the new window." A stained-glass window portraying the Last Supper had been recently installed in Christ Church. Upcountry people came from all over to see it; locals, too.

Eugene returned to the kitchen. "Now what?"

"Church," said Mary Kate, using the rolling pin on the mix.

"What's that got to do with me? I ain't no holy roller."

"No, no, Eugene," said Margaret. "We're talking about Catherine attending services."

"Yes," said Mary Kate, flattening the batter. "She must have the proper clothing, gloves, and a hat."

"Well, she had a suitcase when she arrived. I'm sure there's something in it." Eugene eyed the dough. "Looks like I'm in time for biscuits."

Helen placed the cast iron skillet on the stove. "You two take Catherine upstairs and see what you can come up with. Ask Mrs. Lee, if you must."

Margaret left with Allison, but Mary Kate remained behind. "Who's to help with breakfast?"

Helen looked at Eugene, but the hired man held up his hands. "I'm no cook."

Mary Kate turned over the biscuit cutter. "Food always tastes better when you've had a hand in its preparation." And she disappeared through the doorway to the main house.

"Now that's hooey if I ever heard it." Still, Eugene took down an apron, strapped it on, and began to cut biscuits. After a moment or two, he cleared his throat. "You know, Miss Helen, you promised you'd teach me how to make those brownies."

When Helen didn't reply, Eugene continued to cut out biscuits. It was the odor of burning bacon that caught his attention.

"Miss Helen!"

Helen's head snapped up and she jerked the skillet from the stove. "Sorry, Eugene. Guess I drifted off."

Drifted off to a time when she was closer to Allison's age. Maybe that's why she'd been so hard on the girl. You cry long enough, and you finally learn tears can't do the job. For her, that had been almost fifty years ago at Blind Switch.

Eleven

What they needed from Catherine were tears of anger and rage, not misery and self-pity. Anger and rage had sustained nineteen-year-old Helen from the very first day the Yankees had ridden onto their plantation.

The Yankees' first order of business had been to destroy the sheds, the servants' quarters, and the barn—all for firewood. Horses were turned loose in the fields and the cotton trampled. Hogs were slaughtered and roasted on spits over fires, and the Belles' horses were piled with household goods and led away, along with the cows.

And bales of cotton—oh, the cotton, the thousands and thousands of dollars' worth of cotton!—up in smoke with the barn. The servants, upon being told they were free to go, went, leaving the sisters alone in a world where the night sky lit up to the east of them as Columbia was burned to the ground.

Sitting on the veranda of the Big House with the

commanding officer of the troop occupying her home, Helen asked, "Why do you treat us so, sir? I understand waging war against our men, but destroying everything in your path—why do you do this?"

"Miss Belle," said the colonel, "the people of the North are a peaceful people, but they will not stand idly by and let you tear this country apart."

"Sir, that still does not answer my question as to why you must burn my home to the ground and leave my sisters and myself homeless and destitute."

"Miss Belle, I don't know where the Confederate soldiers reside, but I can tell you where to find their leaders. They live in these fine homes all across the Confederacy. Destroying these homes will keep your family too busy to lead another insurrection against the United States of America."

Helen swallowed her rage. Her mother had taught her not to be rude to visitors. Besides, Margaret sat on the front porch, leaning against one of the colonnades, watching, listening, and frightened. To Margaret there was no worse bogeyman than a Yankee soldier.

"But," said Helen, fighting back the tears, "it may take generations for the South to recover."

"And, Miss Belle," said the colonel, "that would be much too soon as far as I'm concerned."

Mother had died of typhoid when Father returned from a Yankee prison camp and infected her. It had been up to Helen to hold the family together, especially since Mary Kate busily flirted with the Yankees, the only young men she'd seen in years. Margaret had spent her time playing with dolls in the graveyard where Mother and Father were buried, her back to the men striding around Blind Switch like they owned it.

Blind Switch, a name Mother hated, though that horse race enabled their father to win this property when its former owner found his horse trapped behind Father's mount, wedged between another horse and the railing. The former owner cried foul, but the judge said it was a damned shame when an experienced rider allowed his mount to be caught in a blind switch, and the name stuck.

The Yankees remained for a week, sending out patrols to search for Jefferson Davis, the president of the Confederacy. It was said that Davis had fled to Mexico, where he would continue the war. When the Yankees left, not only was Mary Kate's heart broken by the dashing young lieutenant detailed to burn their home to the ground, but young Margaret couldn't be found.

The house was searched inside and out, even by those left behind to put it to torch, but still no Margaret. Mary Kate turned on her lieutenant, accusing him of frightening her little sister to such a degree that she'd hidden God knows where and wouldn't come out, despite their pleading.

After a cursory walk through the building, the lieutenant told his men to douse their torches and ride for Columbia, where Jeff Davis had been seen. All sorts of rumors spread about Davis. Most turned out to be fanciful, as did this one—he would eventually be captured in South Georgia—but at least the Yankees were gone, and their home at Blind Switch left standing.

When Margaret crawled from her hidey-hole on the second-floor landing, Helen demanded to know if the girl was aware that the Yankees were about to burn the house to the ground.

"But they wouldn't burn the house if they thought I was inside."

The older girls looked at each other, and Mary Kate threw her arms around her younger sister and gave her a big hug.

"Smarter than the whole lot of us," she said.

"Smarter than a bunch of Yankees." Helen glanced down the curving stairs leading to the front doors. "Hide again, Margaret. We don't know if those Yankees will return." And Helen grabbed Mary Kate's shoulder and turned the two of them away from their younger sister.

"What in the world are you doing?" asked Mary Kate.

"This way if the Yankees return, we won't have to lie about the whereabouts of our sister."

Mary Kate stood there for a long moment, then convulsed with laughter. "Oh, my, and you thought I'd taken leave of my senses over that young lieutenant from Michigan."

It took only moments for Helen's arm to slide off, and she, too, burst into laughter. Still, neither sister looked to see which way Margaret had gone, and it was one of the few times laughter was heard inside that house for several months to come.

Twelve

A young woman came down the short hallway and into the kitchen. Tall, slender, yet with ample bosom, hips, and bottom, the woman's neck was thin and her hair piled high upon her head, curls dangling down each side—the typical Gibson Girl. For attending church, she wore a semi-tailored navy suit with a high collar. The broadcloth jacket was simple, and the tab extensions on the plaits ran up over the belt, giving a smart look to the peplum; the collar and cuffs were bright red.

"Oh, my," she said, smiling, "but you two are up early this morning."

The hired man could not help but stare. Victoria Lee had that effect on men, and since she had not yet reached forty, she wore very little makeup.

Mrs. Lee took down an apron. "Oh, Eugene, let me cut those biscuits for you."

"Victoria, please," said Helen. "Eugene is trying to earn his keep."

This was intended as a reminder that those in this household must pay their way, a reality quite impossible for Lee.

"Oh, yes. Well, certainly."

Victoria was unflappable. Among the many things that could devastate a woman, one of the worst had happened to her, yet she soldiered on. Abandoned by her husband eight years ago, Victoria was from a good family in Columbus, Ohio, a family that had not approved of their daughter's marriage to a young man from Charleston. After all, it was the damned South Carolinians who had tried to destroy the Union.

Perhaps the family suspected something Victoria did not. None of Edmund Lee's schemes ever worked, though the man could charm money out of anyone who had yet to do business with him. His latest scheme had started well, a small number of people investing modest sums with Lee's brokerage firm on Laurens Street. Thirty days later, the original investors were paid back their investment plus a twenty percent return. From then on, Lee could not beat off the investors with a stick. They lined up each morning outside his office, begging to be taken in.

Everything went along swimmingly, the later investors providing funds for those wishing to cash in their gains, until an unrelated group of investors in New York City tried to corner the market on shares of the United Copper Company. When this bid failed, the banks providing the backing for the New York scheme suffered runs on their deposits, runs extending to their affiliate members, even those as far away as South Carolina.

When the Knickerbocker Trust Company, New York City's third-largest trust, was allowed to fail, the financial system practically collapsed as vast numbers of people tried to withdraw their deposits. Those investing in Edmund Lee's scheme demanded their money back. There wasn't enough to go around, except for what Lee could abscond with, leaving behind his wife and daughter.

No one blamed Victoria. As a woman, she was not responsible for her husband's financial misdeeds, but she did suffer their consequences. Forced out of her new home in Boyce Lawn, one of the first subdivisions in Greenville, neither Mansion House nor the Ottaray Hotel would allow Victoria and Betty Jean to move in. After all, she and her six-year-old daughter were penniless, and everyone knew her family in Ohio had severed all relations.

That's when Mary Kate stepped in. Over Helen's strenuous objections, Victoria and Betty Jean were allowed to move into Belles Lodging and live free. Helen fumed. If there was one unwritten rule all three sisters adhered to, it was that Yankees would never, ever, reside under their roof again, and Mary Kate had gone and broken their cardinal rule.

Not surprisingly, Victoria Lee became more active in the suffrage movement, the Women's Christian Temperance Union, and a parishioner in Christ Church, Episcopal. In most cases, Lee was the first to volunteer for charity work, as if trying to find a point of leverage where she could regain control of her life or repay the good citizens of Greenville for taking her in.

"If you'd like, Victoria," said Helen, "you can lay out the silverware and napkins and take breakfast upstairs to my brother."

"Why, of course."

Victoria went to the stacks of silverware and started counting the proper number of sets, following that with cloth napkins. While Helen finished the bacon and fried a couple of eggs, Eugene popped the biscuits into the oven, then took the tray to the third floor. No reason for Mrs. Lee to climb all those stairs.

Helen shook her head when Eugene disappeared from the kitchen, but she shook her head more in weariness than irritation. If her sisters thought life was unfair to this fourteen-year-old who'd arrived on their doorstep, they had only to consider Victoria Lee.

As for Helen Belle, any illusions she had were dashed when Mrs. Massey had arrived on the steps of Blind Switch with her two daughters and six grandchildren.

Thirteen

The Yankees had burned out the Masseys and taken all their food, along with their horses, cattle, pigs, and chickens, so the Masseys were walking to Greenville.

"Greenville?" asked Helen. Her sisters stood beside her on the veranda of the Big House.

Mrs. Massey's two daughters looked everywhere but at the Belle sisters. Their children had collapsed on the steps, not having the energy to make it as far as the rocking chairs.

"You'll do no such thing," said Mary Kate, who'd danced with Mrs. Massey's grandson before the young man rode off to war. It was rumored that her grandson had died at Gettysburg during some insane attack with bayonets on a Yankee position. "You'll stay with us. We have plenty of room."

Her daughters looked to their mother, hoping she'd remember they'd been on the road for two days. Passersby could trace the Masseys' trek by the bags abandoned along the way.

Once everyone was fed, the exhausted troupe collapsed into beds or onto pallets at the foot of those beds. Everyone slept but Mrs. Massey, who asked Helen to join her on the veranda.

Their food might be meager and the beds lumpy from recent bayonet searches, but Helen's mother had taught her to be gracious. Helen had no idea how severely her mother's rules would be tested in the coming years. So, while Mary Kate went from one room to the other making sure everyone was comfortable, those in the lumpy beds insisted they'd never felt more welcome. Helen and Mrs. Massey took seats in the rockers, and Helen gaped when the older woman lit a corncob pipe.

"A small diversion, my dear. I hope you won't hold it against an old lady."

"Certainly not!" Helen blushed, thankful that darkness had settled in. A proper woman smoking! The war certainly had changed things.

"Chases away the bugs, too, when you have no cedar wood."

Helen nodded in agreement. At this time of day, Helen would ordinarily mouth the compliments all hostesses paid their visitors' families, asking gentle and undemanding questions to bridge the conversation from the dinner table to when everyone retired for the evening. But there was little food, and the effort to grow it, harvest it, and cook it so exhausted Helen that she could only slump in her chair. She so desperately wanted to drag herself off to bed.

Finally, Massey had her pipe going. "They should've burned you out, child. Nothing good can come of this."

Helen had no answer for that. Her mother had taught her to be courteous, especially to her elders.

Looking around in the darkness—candles were much too valuable to burn—Mrs. Massey added, "I haven't seen any men about. Do you or your sisters have a young gentleman?"

The old woman cackled as she rocked back and forth and sucked on her pipe. "Do you have *any* men who have made their intentions known?"

"I believe you should be having this conversation with my mother."

"Your mother's dead, Helen. You are mistress of Blind Switch, and I wish to inquire as to whether you or your sisters have prospects."

"I don't believe that's your concern, but when the time comes for the banns to be read, you'll learn all about it."

"Yes, yes, of course. But is it true that the young men you and Mary Kate intended to marry died in the war?"

Helen allowed herself to nod. That was true. Charles had died at Bull Run and Francis at Second Manassas.

Mrs. Massey stopped rocking and took the pipe from her mouth. "You must have a man around the house. We didn't, and the Yankees burned everything, stole anything they could find, and insulted my daughters."

Helen's hand was at her mouth. "They didn't—"

Massey waved her off with the pipe. "I would no more admit to anything vulgar than you are admitting to your matrimonial circumstances."

Helen considered this. "We have no men around the house. Even the servants ran off."

"Then move to Greenville. Your brother and his wife own a home there."

Helen looked into the darkness. "If we're being forthright, I should mention that we're not on the best of terms with Theresa, and John has yet to return from the war."

Massey puffed on her pipe. "I'm sorry to hear that, since your relationship will only worsen now that you are Theresa's poor relations."

"Us Theresa's poor relations?" Helen leaned back in her rocker and chuckled. "I hardly think so."

"But you have no men to defend your honor, no one to pick your cotton, and little cash money, unless I miss my guess."

A pang of fear struck Helen's heart. She stopped rocking. What this old woman said was true, and she had yet to figure out how she, Mary Kate, and little Margaret would be able to run this plantation. They had found chickens and a rooster in the woods, along with a sow and her litter, but they had no horses or cows. If a baby were on the property, what would they do for milk? What would they do for anything?

"Taxes must be paid in Yankee dollars," said Mrs. Massey, "not Confederate scrip. If you don't have a husband or a father to apply at the bank for a loan—if they'd loan money to anyone in this day and age—I don't know what you and your sisters will do." Massey shot a look at Helen. "Unless you sent your money overseas before the blockade was established."

"Father bought bonds. He said it was our duty to

support the Confederacy." Helen canted her rocking chair around to face the older woman. "What, exactly, are you proposing?"

After another pull on the pipe, Mrs. Massey said, "I always got along well with your family. I danced under this very roof as a young woman." Massey looked down the porch into the darkness. "I met my husband at one of your family barbecues."

"I did not know that."

"He tried to kiss me on this very porch, but I was having none of that. I'd been raised to be a lady. Now life has come full circle. I'm sitting on your porch again, and once again, I'm disappointing someone. I would not wish any harm to befall you or your sisters." Mrs. Massey looked away. "I would not like to happen to you what happened to my girls."

Helen remembered that her two daughters, now widows, had appeared anxious despite their long, exhausting walk. Nervous Nellies is what her mother would've called them. Nowadays, everyone was nervous.

"Why didn't you go into Augusta or Columbia?" asked Helen. "Why Greenville?"

"Columbia is no more. Sherman burned it to the ground, and I've never cared for Georgians. No, my dear, it was either Greenville or Spartanburg, and in Greenville I think we'll have a better chance of finding lodging."

"Your family may remain with us as long as you like."

"Until your food runs out."

"Yes," said Helen, smiling, "there is that small matter."

"No small matter for a woman with six grandchildren. We'll take advantage of your hospitality only for a short while, my dear, until my feet recover; then we must move on to Greenville, which I understand was untouched by the war. Quite a few Unionists live there, so there should be plenty of people who'll take pity on us, if only to make them feel superior to those of us who fought on the losing side."

The Masseys did move on, walking down Stage Road with the few bags they could still carry. Once they disappeared from sight, Helen called Mary Kate and Margaret together to discuss the issues raised by Mrs. Massey.

Mary Kate laughed off the seriousness of their plight. Men were always coming to Mary Kate's rescue, and that would happen again as returning veterans passed this way.

Margaret insisted that they could not leave behind the cemetery where their mother and father were buried. That's why she'd hidden in the house when the Yankees threatened to burn it to the ground. No, said Margaret, shaking her head. She would not leave her mother and father for some unfamiliar home in Greenville.

Helen suggested hanging sheets from the windows, signaling passersby that the inhabitants suffered from cholera. "That should keep the soldiers away."

Mary Kate rejected this out of hand. "Much too cruel."

But when the returning Confederates literally ate them out of house and home, the sisters packed their bags, hung sheets from the roof warning of cholera, and shuttered their house.

After a wistful look back, they headed for Greenville—and the hell of living under the same roof with their sister-in-law. The situation only became grimmer when John returned from war with most of his face shot off.

Fourteen

The deputy from Spartanburg County was in Campobello checking on members of the McKelvey clan when he heard the news: Billy Laughlin was found hanging from the same bridge where the McKelvey family had crashed through the railing and ended up in the river.

"Well," said the farmer who had been brought the news by another McKelvey, "that lets me off the hook. I've been with my family all morning at church."

"Billy's only one of them. There's three more."

The farmer studied him. "Just what the devil are you doing?"

The lawman looked toward Glassy Mountain, a mountain named for the winter sunlight that reflected off its ice and snow.

"You know, Mr. McKelvey, I don't rightly know."

A half hour later, the deputy arrived at the bridge over the ravine. The railing from the Friday evening crash had been repaired, and if there had been a rope tied to the bridge, it had been removed. Billy's body lay in an open wagon covered by a tarp.

Recognizing the wagon as belonging to Earl Laughlin, the deputy blocked the dirt road, got down from his pickup, and walked to where the two brothers were ready to drive off.

The deputy pulled back the tarp and examined the body. Seeing the bruising and rope marks, he threw the tarp over Billy and stepped to the driver's seat. Andrew sat on the far side of the seat, Earl with the reins in his hands.

"What happened here?" he asked.

Andrew leaned over where he could see him. "I'm getting sick and tired of you sticking your nose into our business."

Out of the corner of his eye, the deputy saw the Greenville County sheriff ambling in his direction. Before the sheriff reached him, he asked, "And Billy's reason for hanging himself would be?"

"Gambling debts," said the brothers in unison and looking straight ahead.

"So, this is not a show of remorse on Billy's part?"

Both men continued to stare straight ahead.

"Earl, how much did your brother owe you?"

"It wasn't just me," said Earl, looking down at him from the seat. "Billy owed lots of people. He owed Cleve two hundred fifty-six dollars and ten cents."

"How much did you say?"

Andrew leaned forward again. "Two hundred fifty-six dollars and ten cents."

"Happy to hear you have your stories straight. Sooner

or later, you'll be able to convince yourselves that the McKelvey family *did* die in an accident."

"What you doing over here?" asked the Greenville County sheriff when he reached Earl's wagon.

The deputy from Spartanburg County gestured at the body in the wagon bed. "Family."

Andrew snorted.

"Could you move your truck?" asked Earl, the reins still in his hands.

The deputy started to walk away, then turned and faced the two men on the seat. "How much did Billy owe you, Earl?"

Andrew smiled from beside his brother. "Twenty-three dollars, forty-three cents."

That afternoon, the deputy found Cleve Laughlin playing cards in the smoke-filled back room of the roadhouse. The woman with her hair swept up and her lips painted bright red slept with her head on the blackjack table. The deputy dropped some money on the poker table. All four of the players looked up.

The man in the cowboy hat asked, "What's that for?"

"It's twenty-three dollars and forty-three cents."

"Yeah?" asked Cleve, eyes narrowing.

"I went over to Billy's and told his wife Billy owed me twenty-three dollars and forty-three cents, and the debt was forgiven because of his death. You know what that woman did?"

"If I cared about what women thought, I'd have one hanging around my place."

"I've been to your place. You need one hanging around."

"Mind getting to the point? We're playing cards here."

"Billy's family only has that one room in their cabin."

"I've been there," said Cleve.

"Well, Billy's wife goes over behind a curtain where they sleep, and a few minutes later she comes back and counts out the money. She says she wants all Billy's debts paid."

"So?"

"I ask her how many people had come calling, saying Billy owed them money, and she says nobody, so I ask how come Billy hangs himself? She says she has no idea, but Billy had been acting strange lately. How lately? I ask. She thinks for a minute, then says, 'Over the weekend.' She says she figured he'd get around to telling her what he'd done sooner or later."

The deputy looked around the table. "In case you're thinking of cashing in like I did, Billy and his wife always paid cash. They had no debts." He gestured at the money on the table. "Make sure Billy's widow gets that. I'm sure you and your cousins can come up with a reason, even one that reinforces the idea that Billy's death was actually a suicide."

Fifteen

When Allison came downstairs, she took the steps cautiously, as if expecting someone to grab her and pitch her into the foyer below. She stopped, took a breath, and let it out.

Nothing like that would happen. She was safe. At least that's what two of the three old maids had drummed into her while brushing her hair and fitting her into a dress. That, and who she was. Trying to remember everything could give you a headache.

Allison took another breath and let it out. Mary Kate had spent considerable time in the toilet using a damp cloth on her tear-stained eyes. It seemed to have worked. The red around her eyes had disappeared. These three old women seemed to know a good bit about appearances, physical and otherwise, and had cautioned her about any missteps.

Below her in the foyer sat another test she would eventually have to pass. On a four-foot, solid oak church pew sat a brown-haired girl wearing a bright yellow dress with a matching bow in her curly hair. Her socks came to mid-calf. She held the latest issue of *Harper's Magazine for Young People.*

She looked up when Allison stopped on the stairs. "That's my dress you're wearing."

Allison held onto the railing and examined the light blue pinafore she wore over a white chemise. Her hair was parted in the middle and held in place at the sides with matching bows.

"Want it back?" she asked.

The brown-haired girl dropped the magazine on the pew. She appeared to be the same age as Allison but shorter. On the plus side, the girl had her bosom and a head full of curls.

"No," said the girl. "You may keep the dress. My mother taught me to be generous."

Allison finished the stairs and remembered to curtsy, though she didn't know if she was to curtsy to other girls or not. But this girl did have her bosom, and in social ranking that counted for something.

"What's your name? Mine's Betty Jean Lee."

"I'm Al . . . Catherine Belle."

Betty Jean didn't appear to hear the mistake. "Is it true you're from New Orleans?"

"You don't think so?" asked Allison, becoming defensive again.

It was Allison's first contact with someone who didn't care what her response was. "When my daddy returns, he's going to take me to New Orleans for Mardi Gras. We might go next year."

When all she got was a blank stare, Betty Jean added, "You know, the celebration of Fat Tuesday."

Allison didn't know what Fat Tuesday was, but whatever Tuesday people celebrated being fat, not only would she not qualify but neither would this girl. Both of them were too thin.

"But I wouldn't imagine that they'll hold Mardi Gras next year because of the hurricane, so I guess my father and I will have to go some other time. I've never been in a hurricane. What's it like? I'm not prying about how your family died, but I would like to know if you think my father should take me to see a hurricane."

Allison was not well read, but she'd gotten the impression from the Belle sisters that a hurricane was not a good thing, and here this girl was, rattling along about wanting to go to a hurricane, or Mardi something, or celebrating being fat on Tuesdays. Before she could bolt upstairs and tell the old maids that she couldn't do this, Robert Patton came out of his room. The middle-aged man wore a dark suit, white shirt, and removable high-band collar with the popular lock-front. No tie.

Shutting the door to his room, he noticed the girls. "Why," he said, smiling, "don't you two look lovely."

Swinging her feet while sitting on the pew, Betty Jean said, "That's my dress. I'm letting Catherine wear it."

Patton looked at Allison. "How nice." He glanced at the grandfather clock in the foyer and saw one of the hands reaching for the bottom of the hour. "Well, time for church."

"We're waiting for my mother. She went upstairs to get Uncle John's dishes."

"And Margaret?"

Allison realized Patton was asking her. "Oh . . . sir, she's upstairs . . . getting dressed. Sir."

"Well, I don't think we should be discussing . . ." Patton cleared his throat. "I'll just wait . . . outside."

"Aunt Mary Kate is with her," continued Allison. "We're going to church. We belong to Christ Church on Church Street."

Maybe that was a bit too much information, but Allison didn't know when to stop. "In New Orleans, we attended a French Huguenot church." Oh, my, what if someone asked her what a French Huguenot was? She didn't remember, and Huguenots were simply Huguenots, not French, that much she recalled.

"I'll wait outside." Patton took out a cigar as he headed for the door.

Betty Jean reminded Patton that Margaret Belle did not care much for cigars.

Hand on the knob, Patton turned and stared at the child on the pew. "Er . . . yes," he said before going out.

Once the door closed behind him, Betty Jean said, "Mr. Patton is writing a history of Greenville District. That's what Greenville was called before the Yankees changed its name." Betty Jean lowered her voice conspiratorially. "He has a crush on your aunt Margaret."

"He does?" Allison didn't know what that meant.

"At least that's what Mother believes. It's all in how a man handles himself around a particular woman."

Thankfully, Allison was saved from more questions by two grumbling salesmen coming downstairs. The two men ignored the girls and went out the door. Behind the traveling salesmen came two of Allison's aunts. Both wore flowery dresses, low heels, and hats adorned with ribbons, lace, and veils.

The grandfather clock signaled the half hour.

Allison jumped.

"Silly," laughed Betty Jean, "haven't you heard a grandfather clock before?"

"Er . . . just not here." Before Betty Jean could pepper her with another question, Allison said, "I'm not used to one in the hallway."

"Lots of people have clocks in their foyers. That's how the family tells time."

Allison noticed the wider-than-usual entrance leading to the room across the hallway. "The parlor! That's where we had our grandfather clock. In New Orleans. I lived in New Orleans."

"When we lived in Boyce Lawn, we owned a grandfather clock."

Allison's puzzled look caused Betty Jean to explain.

"It's on the other side of Christ Church. A very nice section of town, but we don't live there with Father gone. Too much house to keep up." She glanced toward the dining room. "I wonder whether you'll sit above or below the salt."

Victoria Lee came down with John Belle's tray. "Catherine will probably sit at the children's table with you, my dear."

Betty Jean let her mother know that she was too sophisticated to sit at a table with children. Besides, she and Catherine were the only children in the house.

Catching up with the two old maids coming down the stairs, Victoria added, "We're guests in these people's home, Betty Jean, and you're setting the wrong tone."

"Nonsense," said Margaret Belle, reaching the bottom of the stairs, "you're practically family."

Still, Victoria shot her daughter a severe look before disappearing into the kitchen with the tray.

"I see you've met Betty Jean," said Mary Kate, pulling on her gloves. "That should give you someone with whom to share secrets."

"Mary Kate, do you know how that sounds?"

"Margaret, dear, Catherine knows I wasn't encouraging her to be indiscreet."

Allison merely stood there. She had no idea what anyone was talking about, but she understood Betty Jean Lee. Allison didn't need to understand the girl's words, just their tone.

"I don't know if I have any secrets," said Allison, "but if I think of one, I'll make sure I share it with my new friend."

At this, everyone smiled, several in relief.

✣ ✣ ✣

Helen looked up from preparing Sunday dinner and saw the three of them file into the kitchen. She did not remember hearing the grandfather clock signal the half hour, much less the hour, but time did get away from her preparing meals, or cleaning up after them.

"What's this?" she asked, glancing at the clock.

"She couldn't stop crying," said Mary Kate.

Helen gave the red-eyed Allison a look, but the girl only stood at the end of the preparation table and stared at the floor.

"Attending church reminded Catherine of her family,"

explained Margaret, "and the funeral she won't be able to attend."

Helen wiped her hands on her apron. "I'm sorry to hear that, but I have little sympathy for the child."

"She lost her family," said Margaret, as if this explained all.

"Yes," said Mary Kate, "even that didn't happen to us. We still had each other."

In the hallway, the clock bonged the half hour.

"I'll be right back." Helen untied her apron. "You two get to work on dinner. Both the chicken and the ham are ready to come out of the oven." The midday meal was always served at two.

"Where are you going?" asked Margaret.

"To call the sheriff." The phone was on a table in the foyer.

"Why do we need the sheriff?"

"Because Allison can put the Laughlins in jail for what they did to her family and she needs to speak her piece before she forgets the tiniest detail."

"They'll kill her. There's too many of them."

"One of the Spartanburg deputies is a Laughlin."

At the doorway, Helen faced them. "I told you this wouldn't work, and it's best we stop fooling ourselves before we put this household in further jeopardy."

"But you can't do this!"

"I'm sorry, Margaret, but I won't lose this house over someone who's lost their nerve."

Margaret glanced at Allison cowering on the other side of the table. To her oldest sister, she said, "This is wrong! You can't do this! I won't let you."

"And neither will I," said Mary Kate. "The girl has no

one to turn to. We'll take a vote."

"No vote was taken about her moving in."

"I . . . I had to do it," stammered Margaret.

"You have only her word that she doesn't have any relatives. The sheriff will learn if that's true or not."

"It's our Christian duty to provide for this girl."

"Just as it is her Christian duty to attend church Sundays."

"Give her some time."

"She doesn't have time, and neither do we. By shielding her from the Laughlins, we're hindering prosecution of a crime."

"Oh, Helen," said Mary Kate, with a lift to her voice, "you're quite the lawyer."

"The sheriff knows the law. Question him."

Mary Kate lost her smile. "You're serious!"

"You want to risk this house for some stranger?"

"Catherine's no stranger," said Margaret, finding her voice. "She's part of our family now."

"And when we're thrown out, she'll provide for us. After all, men like their mistresses young, not some old maid."

"Oh, my goodness," said Mary Kate, hand coming up to her throat, "don't be so crude."

"Then marry her off to a rich man, or am I to expect my reward in heaven? Or prison?"

"We're not going to be thrown out of this house," said Mary Kate, an edge coming into her voice.

"That's a chance you're willing to take?"

The sisters were still arguing when Allison cut through them, heading down the short hallway and returning to the main house.

"Where are you going, my dear?" called Mary Kate. She tried to put some lightness in her voice.

"Back to church! Anything's better than this."

The sisters watched her go.

"You know," said Mary Kate, "I think Catherine's going to fit right into this family."

The second time Allison left for church she heard a bugle blowing. Outside, she stopped on the porch and gawked at five soldiers wearing butternut uniforms, really old men, all but one on horseback. The fifth soldier was raising a flag Allison had seen on the wall of her home. It was the sovereign flag of the state of South Carolina, a blue St. George's Cross on a red field, fifteen white stars on the blue cross, and on the red field in the upper left corner, palmetto and crescent symbols. Called the "secession" flag, it was flown not only in the South but also by Northerners who supported the South during the Civil War.

Allison had noticed the flagpole in the front yard, but until now there had been no flag. She stopped at the edge of the porch and watched the flag being raised and listened as a bugler on horseback played reveille. The other four men saluted.

Up and down West Washington a small crowd had gathered. Several men wore suits, and more than one wore the same butternut uniform as the old men on horseback. The men in suits and the women accompanying them held a hand across their heart; those in uniform saluted. Among those she recognized was the policeman who had escorted her from the train depot to Belles Lodging. He stood ramrod straight, saluting a flag treasured by the members of Allison's own family. Next to him stood more policemen, several firemen, and a couple of members of the sheriff's department.

When reveille ended, one of the men on horseback called an order, and the men dropped their salute. The soldier who had raised the flag remounted his horse and another command was shouted. The horses wheeled a quarter turn.

One of the soldiers saw Allison staring up at him. Excited to see soldiers on horseback and to hear the bugler play, Allison had wandered down the steps to the street. For the first time in two days, she felt alive, even joyous. The music and the flag called to her.

"Who are you," demanded the soldier, "to interfere in these solemn proceedings?"

"Allison McKelvey."

Every soldier's head turned in her direction.

The old man cocked his. "Allison McKelvey, you say?"

She glanced at her new family on the porch, then faced the soldier again. "Yes, sir, I truly am."

The elderly man grinned down at her. "The same Allison McKelvey who died at Guilford Courthouse?"

Remembering what the Laughlins had done to her family, Allison stuck out her chin and said, "I'm not dead yet, sir."

The old man extended a hand. "Allison McKelvey belongs on horseback, not afoot. He was the greatest horseman produced by the Revolutionary War."

Allison swung up into the saddle in front of him, and as they rode through downtown, Allison felt she was finally home.

Sixteen

It was dusk when Allison returned to Belles Lodging with the Confederate soldiers. People in rocking chairs rose to their feet and those standing in small groups across the street faced the flag once again. Hands across hearts for the civilians; those in uniform held their salute until the flag was lowered, folded, and tucked under one of the soldiers' arms while the bugler played retreat.

At the conclusion of retreat, the soldiers doffed their hats to Allison, and she returned the favor with a curtsy. Then the elderly men rode off in single-file formation, heading in the direction of old Camp Wetherill.

With the phrase "There's Johnny boy!" ringing in her ears, Allison looked to the third-floor turret. All she could see was the head of a man sitting in a chair. Drifting through the front windows of Belles Lodging came the sound of Enrico Caruso on the Victrola and Robert Patton taking another rubber in bridge.

Two of her "aunts" were waiting on the porch when

Allison came up the steps. Betty Jean Lee was there, too, bursting with questions, but her mother's hand on her shoulder caused the girl to hold her tongue. A curt "Good evening" was all the lodgers received from Mary Kate and Margaret as they marched their "niece" through the house and out to the kitchen. There, they were soon joined by Helen adjusting her glasses on her nose.

As the older of the three sisters came through the kitchen door, Allison threw her arms around her. "Thank you so very much for letting me come live with you, Aunt Helen."

Taken aback, but only for a moment, Helen held the girl out and away from her. "Don't think this is going to get you out of trouble, young lady."

But Allison had moved on to hug her other "aunts" and thank them for taking her in when she had no place to go. Once she had hugged Mary Kate and Margaret, she took a seat on a stool on the far side of the preparation table, hands in her lap, and stared at the tabletop.

Margaret dabbed her eyes with the corner of her apron, and Mary Kate returned to the doorway to stand guard. This was going to get messy, and loud.

"Where have you been?" demanded Helen.

Allison continued to stare at the tabletop. "To say good-bye to my family."

The three women looked at each other. Helen didn't know what to say. Neither did Margaret.

"My dear," asked Mary Kate, "the soldiers took you where?"

Allison looked up. "They planned to ride up State Road to the Saluda Gap."

"The Saluda Gap!" exclaimed Margaret.

"Are you serious?" demanded Helen. "That's all the way up in North Carolina."

"I know, I know. I suggested we ride through the Dark Corner. They seemed to like the idea."

"Oh," laughed Margaret. "They would. That part of the county was a Unionist stronghold during the war."

Mary Kate found herself chuckling. "I'm surprised they didn't come back for their flag."

Helen wasn't amused. "After all we've done, and you go traipsing off to where the Laughlins killed your family." She shook her head. "It makes no sense . . . no sense at all."

Tears started down Allison's cheeks, but she hastily wiped them away. "I'm sorry, but I had . . . I had to see . . ." She gulped. "Someone buried them . . . on our farm. And that's where I've got to leave them." Her shoulders slumped.

"Is there a grave for you, too?" asked Mary Kate from where she stood guard at the door.

"Yes."

"Then that means you belong here with us."

Helen asked, "Am I the only one who sees this as a problem?"

Margaret came around the table and put a hand on Allison's shoulder. "We're just glad you're home safe."

"Yes," said Mary Kate, glancing behind her, then smiling from the doorway, "you had us all worried."

But Helen was irritated. "While you were gone, my sisters made me promise not to inquire through the authorities regarding you or your family, and now you had these men take you home?" The older woman shook her head in disgust.

Allison had been wiping the tears away. "No, no, it's not like that. We just rode around . . . and I acted excited, wanting to see this, wondering where that trail went, or this path. When we were close to my farm, I told them I had to go." She flushed. "I ran off into the woods and . . . found the graves. The veterans think I got lost. Really, Aunt Helen, I didn't give them cause to think I knew my way around. Where I live . . . where I lived is up a hollow. People who don't know their way get lost all the time."

"Those men are lucky someone didn't mistake them for revenuers," said Margaret.

"Not in butternut uniforms, they wouldn't," said Mary Kate. "They'd be shot for being Rebs, not revenuers."

"I know I was rude and disrespectful," continued Allison, "and you have every right to scold me, even take a belt to me, but it was more than I could stand—falling in the river, being in the barn with the neighbors watching, all these people I had to meet, and you want me to be a lady." Tears ran down her cheeks again. "Oh," she said, wiping away the tears with her fingers and throwing them away. "I'm so tired of crying."

Margaret furnished a handkerchief. "No one's going to take a belt to you, Catherine."

"But did you have to tell the soldiers your real name?" asked Helen. "Don't you think that was rather dangerous?"

"Oh," said Allison, wiping away a rebellious tear. "They think I'm a kid who loves to listen to old folks—" She glanced at the tabletop. "I'm sorry. I mean elderly people talk about the war. To them, I'm Katie Belle."

"Katie? Not Catherine?"

"They didn't care much for 'Catherine.'"

"'Catherine' is a perfectly acceptable name," said Helen. "A name that carries much honor in our family."

"Oh, Helen," said Mary Kate, leaving the doorway to join them at the table, "'Katie' is just fine." She reached across the table and took the girl's hands with her own. "Are you hungry, my dear? We had both chicken and ham today."

Margaret headed for the refrigerator. "I'll get the milk. You must be starving."

"Just a moment here," said Helen. "Are you allowing this girl to get off scot-free? She's acted irresponsibly."

"She's not 'this girl.' She's a member of our family."

"And sounds much more grown up than earlier today."

"What did they talk about, my dear?"

"The war. They talked about all these battles."

"That's because none of them fought in combat," said Helen with a sneer.

"They didn't?"

"Men who've fought in combat never talk about it."

"But why raise the flag? Why do you have the flagpole?"

"It's for John. Our brother *did* fight in the war."

"And how would we stop them?" asked Margaret.

Allison was incredulous. "You want to stop the veterans from raising the flag? What harm can come of it? They told me the Federal post office closes on Sundays and that's when the secession flag can fly all day."

"You think we like having a flag-raising ceremony at our house every Sunday?" demanded Helen. "That pole was planted in the middle of the night, and I swear the Klan had a hand in it."

"Those men want to honor Johnny," said Margaret. She stood beside Allison, rubbing the girl's back. "He took the worst of the war and survived."

"Plenty of men who fought in the war came home and contributed to society," said Mary Kate, "but Johnny can't do that, not with his injuries."

"Maybe Uncle John should come down one Sunday and give those men what for," suggested Allison.

The three women looked at each other, trading anxious looks.

Eugene came through the door. "John should do what?"

When no one answered, the hired man said, "I see the girl's back, and no worse for wear. You must have ridden a lot in New Orleans, Catherine."

Allison gave him a broad smile. "Well, Mister Eugene, we lived on a farm outside town. Outside the city, I mean. I guess you can tell by my accent."

"I've never seen a girl ride like a man before." He grinned. "You'll be the talk of school tomorrow."

The old women looked at each other. "School?"

"Yeah. I reckoned you were going to enroll her in Central tomorrow."

The women were stunned. If there was a subject that rarely came up in the Old Maids' Club, it would be Central School.

Eugene slapped his stomach with both hands, then patted it. "Anyway, I figured if you were heating up the leftovers, maybe I could have another slice of that apple pie."

"Of course, Mr. Eugene," said Allison. She reached over and took the dome off the cake plate at the end of the preparation table.

Mary Kate slid a plate across to her. That was followed by a pie knife from Margaret. Deftly, Allison slipped the pie knife under the apple pie and out came a pre-cut slice. She slid the slice onto the plate and slid the plate over to Eugene, who had stuck a napkin in his shirt collar and taken a fork from the rows of silverware on the counter.

While Eugene chewed his first bite, Allison looked up from under her eyebrows and asked, "Do you think, one day, maybe, we might get a horse?"

Seventeen

Monday morning was a blur, and it all began at breakfast when Betty Jean asked if Catherine would be accompanying her to Central School.

Helen answered: "Her aunts will accompany her to school."

It had been determined by the three old maids that their "niece" would attend the public school, that they were not going to throw money away by enrolling her in primary classes at Greenville Woman's College. On this point, Helen was adamant, and the others went along.

Their "niece" was all nerves, and it didn't help that the night before, the sisters had examined her in math, reading, and writing skills to get a better idea of her abilities. Fortunately, Allison's mother had insisted that her daughter learn the three Rs.

"I've read the Bible through twice, and I know the Lord's Prayer and the Twenty-third Psalm by memory."

Mary Kate chuckled. "Having the courage to walk through the valley of the shadow of death and fear no evil—I would assume every child in the Dark Corner can quote that particular Bible verse."

"Aren't you being sacrilegious?" asked Katie.

"Well," said Mary Kate, "maybe just a little."

With a great sense of relief the sisters put their niece to bed Sunday night on a pallet in their room. The girl could read, write, and do her sums. The problem was that when it came to anything outside the church or how to farm she was totally uninformed.

"One of us must be with her at all times," said Helen. "Or this is not going to work."

"I disagree," said Mary Kate. "I think this afternoon with the veterans changed the whole game for Katie."

"Mary Kate," said Helen, "this is not some baseball game. You must take this seriously."

"I take everything seriously, my dear, but if I choose not to belabor a point, that doesn't mean I don't care."

"Are you two going to argue all night. I swear if—"

"Don't swear," said Helen.

The younger sister gritted her teeth. "You know what I mean. You and Mary Kate argue so much there's no time to think."

The older two glared at her.

"Now," said Margaret, ignoring their looks, "what does a girl need when she attends school? She must have pencils and a pad. What books does she need? Perhaps a bag?"

"Eugene has a rucksack from the war," suggested Helen. "She could use that."

"A drab old military bag," said Mary Kate. "Can't we do better than that?"

Margaret's face lit up. "What about letting the children attending Central tell us?"

"What do you mean?"

"Well, we could just go and look."

Mary Kate nodded. "That would work."

"She's going to have books," groaned Helen. "She's going to have to have lots and lots of books. Everyone will be ahead of her. She'll need Dickens, Hugo, the Bronte sisters—"

"And Jane Austen," suggested Mary Kate.

"Austen? Really, my dear, we need something a bit more serious. Next, you'll suggest Sir Walter Scott and Robert Louis Stevenson."

Mary Kate smirked. "Oh, then, Mark Twain for sure."

"Do you have to joke about everything?"

"Only about your primness, my dear."

"Browning and Tennyson," suggested Margaret. "There must be some poets included."

"*Anne of Green Gables,*" added Mary Kate. "The third volume is available, the one where Anne and Gilbert kiss for the first time."

Margaret's hand was at her mouth. "Do you really think we should encourage such activities. We're responsible for this girl."

Mary Kate laughed. "Are you speaking of reading or kissing?"

"You've read *Anne of Green Gables?*" asked Helen. She was, to say the least, incredulous.

Mary Kate shrugged. "Am I to read only James and Chekhov and Conrad? How dreary."

"Who's to take her to Central?" asked Margaret.

"You two," said Helen. "We have lodgers to keep happy. They're the ones I feel a responsibility toward, not some orphan."

So the old maids went to bed when the grandfather clock struck nine. Well, Helen did, knowing her responsibilities would come much earlier in the morning. The other two sisters remained awake, whispering about Katie's potential, and more than once they stared in wonder at the girl sleeping on the pallet, and smiled at the plans they had made for her.

✣ ✣ ✣

When the alarm rang at five, Helen wasn't surprised that her sisters and the girl slept on. Helen pulled on her robe, picked up her vanity case, and went down the hall to the bathroom, open to women until six; men from six until seven.

Victoria and Betty Jean were already there. Victoria always rose early to set the table and take breakfast upstairs to John. By five-thirty, the Belle sisters, Mrs. Lee, and Betty Jean would relinquish the bathroom to any other female lodgers who wished to use the facilities before six. This time of year, however, there were mostly salesmen making their calls before winter set in.

The second-floor bathroom had been added when the new kitchen was built directly beneath it; above, a smaller bath was installed for John. Both were reached by a similar short hallway off the main building. The bathroom on the second floor was almost as large as the kitchen below, with matching lavatories and mirrors.

These flanked a porcelain claw-footed tub with a shower enclosure and sunflower showerhead.

Boarders were encouraged to bathe at night to avoid early morning congestion. The bathroom had no windows and a small electric heater stood against one wall. Above the space heater were rods for towels, though damp towels were expected to dry on rods in each boarder's room. However, as the sisters learned, a towel was always being left behind by some salesman who expected to be picked up after. That never changed.

Betty Jean turned away from a lavatory she shared with her mother and asked Helen, "Where's Catherine?"

"Betty Jean," warned her mother, "that's an adult you're speaking to."

The girl returned to the mirror and finished taking the rag rollers from her hair.

"I'm sorry, Miss Belle," said Victoria. "Betty Jean couldn't sleep last night, planning Catherine's first day at school."

"Neither could my sisters."

"If Catherine needs any additional clothing—"

"I'm sure my sisters will stop by Meyers-Arnold and pick out what she needs." Helen went to the opposite mirror and examined the damage from last night. "But we appreciate all you've done."

A thought struck Helen. "Betty Jean, would you like to go down the hall and wake up Katie and make sure she's ready for school on time?"

The girl was confused but excited. "Katie?"

"Catherine goes by 'Katie' now. Maybe you could . . ."

Helen's voice trailed off as Betty Jean raced from the bathroom, leaving the door open. Her mother tightened her robe, stepped to the door, and shouted at her daughter about her rudeness, but Betty Jean was gone, skipping down the hall to the old maids' bedroom.

Victoria tried to apologize.

"Think nothing of it," said Helen. "She's excited about having another young person in the house."

Helen followed Betty Jean out of the bathroom, closing the door behind her. In the short hallway that separated the bath from the main house, she knocked on a door next to the bathroom. When no objection came, she opened the door to a small room where the toilet was located. Minutes later, she returned to the main bath and found Catherine pulling a hairbrush through her dark hair.

Katie smiled into the mirror. "Morning, Aunt Helen."

Those were about the last words Katie spoke to Helen up to the moment the girls, Mary Kate, Margaret, and Victoria left to catch the trolley. The girls were so deep in discussion about what Central was like that Katie paid little attention to their mode of travel: another kind of train.

The trolley stopped at the head of McBee Avenue, and Betty Jean leapt to the ground and raced away before realizing that some boy might be watching. A tentative Katie Belle eased herself from the trolley. She, too, saw boys wearing suits with full-length trousers or cut off above the knee, and while Betty Jean made the prospect sound delightful, Katie wasn't so sure. She'd never had a boyfriend before, but her new friend made it sound like the most normal thing in the world.

While she waited for her aunts to be assisted to the street by the conductor, Katie saw children climbing out of automobiles, tangles of wiring overhead for telephone, electric, and trolley car service, and in front of her, Central School, a two-story building with ten grades and almost a thousand students.

Over the din of students' chatter, Betty Jean wished Katie good luck and headed off to her eighth-grade classroom. Because of Mrs. Lee's efforts, and the fact that she lived in a boarding house surrounded by adults, Betty Jean was performing at a level higher than her age group. Katie, on the other hand, after being examined by the headmaster, was sent to sit with the students in sixth grade.

Mary Kate and Margaret were mortified by this placement, and after reminding Katie that they still loved her and insisting that she would soon catch up, the two old maids returned to Belles Lodging. There, they sat at the other side of the preparation table and sulked while their older sister sliced potatoes. All the leftovers from Sunday dinner would be dumped in the pot, along with the potatoes, for the evening meal.

Helen held up her knife to make a point. "How long is this girl to be here? Do we even know?"

Margaret did not look at Helen, only shook her head.

Mary Kate said, "She's not this girl but our niece."

"Uh-huh," said Helen.

Margaret asked, "How is Katie to learn how to speak properly if you don't."

Her sister shook the knife at her. "Don't try to change the subject."

"It wouldn't matter. She's still a child of God and we have a responsibility to her."

"Now you sound like President Wilson."

Mary Kate interrupted their bickering. "I assume you believe Catherine should perform chores."

Gesturing with the knife at a pad lying on the counter behind her, Helen said, "There's the list. I made it up as I thought of it."

Margaret left her seat, went around the table, and picked up the pad. Mary Kate remained on her stool opposite her older sister.

She said, "Helen, I think we should rethink Catherine's chores. They may not be the proper ones for her situation."

Margaret held up the pad. "This is totally unrealistic."

Helen sighed and returned to slicing another potato. "The girl had it worse living on a farm."

That stopped Margaret but not Mary Kate.

"Helen," asked Mary Kate, "what if the list is wrong?"

Her sister dropped the sliced potatoes in the pot. "You haven't even looked at the list."

"I don't have to."

Margaret tried to hand the pad across the table, but Mary Kate refused it.

Helen saw this. "I don't want to fight. I've been busy washing dishes while you two have been off tilting at windmills."

Mary Kate straightened up on her stool. "I'm calling court into session."

Helen put down the knife. "I don't have time for this."

Margaret asked, "What do you want to adjudicate?"

"Catherine's chores."

Margaret slid the pad across the table. "Perhaps you'd better review this list before you ask for a hearing."

"As I said, I don't need to see the list."

Helen put both hands palm down on the table, leaned over, and glared at her sister. "Then present your argument."

"Catherine is deficient in her studies—on that we all agree."

"But she still must do chores. All children do. Even Betty Jean. Her mother makes Betty Jean keep their room in tip-top condition, even has the girl clean the bathroom once a week. Betty Jean gets to choose the day, but she does clean the bathroom."

"I don't understand . . ." started Margaret.

Helen held up a hand. "This is between Mary Kate and me."

"I don't want to see you two fight over this girl." Margaret's voice trailed off as her two older sisters turned on her. "Okay, okay, court's in session."

"More slang." Returning her attention to Mary Kate, Helen made a come-along motion. "Give."

"It's simple. During the war when soldiers reported to Camp Wetherill, the volunteers had to participate in some sort of basic training. The idea was to have them perform as a unit. A group of civilians could not be turned into a fighting force without this rudimentary training. It was a concentrated effort to bring the volunteers up to the level of regular army personnel."

"It didn't always work," noted Helen.

Margaret clapped her hands together, excited. "I

see where you're going. You think Katie needs basic training for school."

Mary Kate nodded. "In everything she needs assistance: behavior, education, and especially table manners. You saw how she ate this morning."

"But she still must have chores."

"Maybe her chores are to learn how to be a lady, or practice penmanship, or adopt the rules of decorum."

Margaret nodded. "And the more she knows, the less chance someone will recognize her as Allison McKelvey."

"Wait a minute," said Helen, "you want us to play Henry Higgins to Catherine's Eliza Doolittle?"

"I'm only suggesting that Catherine needs several weeks of intense training in how to fit into modern-day society. It's going to be difficult enough to keep up her studies, and naturally she wants to spend time with Betty Jean."

"In other words," grumbled Helen, "no chores."

"There could be chores, and whoever is minding her, that particular sister could work her brain as we work her hands."

"And if I don't miss my guess," added Margaret, "Katie is going to feel awfully disappointed at being placed in the sixth grade with those younger children. Besides, she's tall for her age."

"That should open her mind to the amount of work that needs to be done," said Mary Kate.

"Yes, yes," said Margaret, picking up her purse and heading for the short hallway. "I'll walk over to the Woman's College and learn what studies Katie should master before graduating from Central."

"You're planning on sending her to college?" asked Helen.

"Why not?" asked Margaret. "It's just down the street."

Helen could not believe what she was hearing. What was wrong with her sisters? They were no more responsible for this girl than the man in the moon was.

Katie surprised them by returning home in the custody of Mrs. Lee well before school let out. The sisters were washing and drying dishes from the midday meal when Victoria escorted Katie into the kitchen. Her dress was torn and dirty, as were her stockings; her hair in a state.

Katie had been sent home for fighting—but not with the sixth graders. She had beaten up two eighth grade boys who were jealous of her exalted status. Neither of the boys had ever been invited to ride with Confederate veterans.

Helen Belle laced into Katie for fighting, Mary Kate lectured her for her unladylike behavior, but Margaret only shook her head and tore up the course of study provided by the dean of the Woman's College.

Eighteen

"Those boys called me a 'Dirty Reb.'"

"Sticks and stones," warned Margaret.

"What were the boys' names?"

Victoria told them.

"Well," said Helen Belle, "to those boys, you *are* a dirty Reb. They're both from Unionist families."

"If you'll excuse me," said Victoria, whose roots were in Ohio. "I must be going."

Mary Kate glanced at the clock ticking on the wall. "Thank you for what you've done, Victoria. I hope this doesn't make you late for your other duties."

"Oh," said Victoria, smiling, "it's one of the perquisites of assisting at the phone company. I can call from here and warn them that I'll be running a bit late."

"You could've called from Central," said Helen. "I would've come over and brought the girl home."

"Oh, yes, well. I must be going." Victoria left the kitchen.

Once Victoria was gone, Margaret said, "You see,

Katie, you've embarrassed Mrs. Lee. She helps out at the school every morning. She's a great resource for Central."

"And you've made her late for her shift at the phone company," added Helen.

As Margaret took eggs and butter from the refrigerator and passed them across the table to Mary Kate, the youngest sister said, "Mrs. Lee fills in for the operator at Southern Bell during lunch."

"You won't make many friends acting out," said Mary Kate, placing the eggs and butter beside the flour and the shortening. She was preparing to mix a pound cake, a lodgers' favorite.

On her side of the preparation table, Katie sulked. "A lot of children said I did good."

"Did *well.*" Mary Kate turned from the stove. "For fighting?"

"No. For winning!"

Again they stared at the girl.

Helen was the first to break the silence. "So what do we have here? We're a family of dirty Rebs and our so-called niece has insulted two of the most prominent families in Greenville."

"So-called niece?" asked Mary Kate.

"That's just plain hurtful," said Margaret.

Mary Kate smiled across the table. "You see how fast people can turn on you, my dear."

Helen ignored the crack. "Catherine, I want you to march upstairs, bathe, and put on the nicest dress Betty Jean lent you."

"But I never bathe until Saturday."

"We have water in this house, young lady, and you'll

bathe when I tell you." Helen motioned for Katie to dismount the stool. "Let's go, young lady! Get those spirits up! We're going shopping."

"Her reward for fighting is a trip to Efird's?" asked Mary Kate, smirking. "Who do I have to smack?"

"Mary Kate, please, no slang."

Katie was happily confused, but that was cut off by her aunt Helen. "Don't get your hopes up, Catherine. When I'm through with you, you'll think twice about fighting. Hopefully, the boys will think twice about it, too."

"I'll be happy to go along."

"Nice try, Margaret. Just make sure she's clean, and wash behind her ears. And call the hairdresser to have her come over. You'll need some foundation to cover that black eye. And find Betty Jean's copy of *Rebecca of Sunnybrook Farm.* Do you have any clean undergarments, Catherine?"

Katie shook her head.

Again, Helen turned to Margaret. "While Catherine's in the tub, call Victoria at Southern Bell and ask permission to enter her room and find clean underwear and a chemise."

"Wow," said Mary Kate, "you're really making her over."

"From the skin up," said Helen, walking to the kitchen window. "That's all I can do. The rest is up to her."

Helen leaned over the two sinks and rapped on the glass, drawing Eugene's attention. The hired man was changing the oil in the Buick. She motioned him inside. He nodded and wiped his hands on a rag as he headed for the back door.

"I'm sending my card to those two families. Hopefully, they'll see us and accept our apologies."

Margaret was ushering Katie out of the kitchen. She stopped and asked, "Let me see if I have this correct: Catherine's to apologize for winning?"

"Oh, it'll be much worse," said Helen, smiling wickedly. "When Catherine and I finish rehearsing, she'll be able to convince both mothers, and hopefully their sons, that Catherine didn't win any fights, but the boys tripped and fell, and she took unfair advantage of them while they were on the ground."

"But that's not true!" protested Katie from the doorway where she stood next to Margaret. "I whupped them fair and square."

Mary Kate tried to correct the girl's language.

"Not now, Mary Kate." To Katie, Helen said, "I will not have tomboys living in this house. Betty Jean had to learn that, and you shall too." Helen gestured at the window. "Otherwise, you can sleep in the carriage house."

By this time Eugene had come through the back door, and Margaret, Mary Kate, and Katie had disappeared into the front of the house.

"What now?" he asked.

"Wash your hands and face, comb your hair, and put on a jacket." She told him where to take the cards.

"Putting on airs, are we? That wasn't part of the bargain when I hired on."

"It becomes part of the bargain when you have a young woman in the house, so you may as well get used to it. Otherwise, pack your belongings and be out of here within the hour."

"No reason to be huffy. I still need to put in the new oil."

"I'm not in a huff, and if you must know, this is all my sisters' doing."

"Then put your foot down."

"Sorry. I lost the vote."

Heading for the back door, Eugene shook his head and grumbled. "I never did understand all that voting."

"The easiest way of dealing with women who've yet to be enfranchised."

Scrubbed clean, Katie was turned over to the hairdresser, who set up shop in the bathroom. The result would be a bun on the top of Katie's head with a few curls down each side.

"How'd you get that shiner, young lady?" asked the hairdresser, a short, thick woman.

"Oh, it's nothing," said Margaret with an embarrassed laugh. "Catherine ran into a door."

The hairdresser returned her attention to the girl. It was no business of hers what went on behind the closed doors of such a prim and proper household as the Belles', but in the hairdresser's world, running into a door translated into child beating.

After receiving her bun and a bit of foundation for the shiner, Katie set off with Helen for Meyers-Arnold.

The department store, specializing in women's and children's clothing, had been purchased by the Meyers brothers of Newport News, Virginia, only a few years earlier. Things were looking up for consumers in Greenville. Monied interests that had formerly invested in building warships at Hampton Roads were investing some of that money in Greenville. Belk-Kirkpatrick of Charlotte planned to open a store just down the street the following year.

An hour later, Katie appeared on Main Street wearing a sporty pink skirt and a white cotton blouse. Accessorized with a matching pink tie, all in all, the outfit gave Katie the appearance of preparing for a game of croquet, not a wrestling match. Men looked her way, and Katie noticed.

"Oh," she said, as packages were stacked in the passenger's seat of the Belles' touring car diagonally parked at the curb. Eugene held open the back door, and Katie followed her aunt into the car, taking a seat in the rear. "I remember this from the barn."

Helen shot the girl a look.

Eugene didn't appear to make the connection. He had his own agenda. "Your aunt Helen is putting on airs, Catherine." The Belles' hired man wore a jacket and had his hair combed and slicked back with petroleum jelly.

Helen looked around. "Now, where is that book?"

Eugene took *Rebecca of Sunnybrook Farm* from the front seat and handed it to Helen. "I don't think this is my kind of story."

"I didn't know you read novels, Eugene."

"Only the good stuff: Zane Grey, Owen Wister, Ned Buntline."

"Ned Buntline? Wasn't he an outlaw?"

"No, ma'am. He commissioned the Buntline Special from the Colt Manufacturing Company and gave it to Wyatt Earp."

"The Earp Brothers, now, I know *they* were outlaws. They shot people at the OK Corral."

"Oh, Miss Helen, I see I have my work cut out for me."

Around them, motor cars were the predominant form of transportation, but here and there plodded a carriage, usually in the employ of some farmer who'd come to town to buy a motor car. Many dealerships thrived in the West End, a sort of mile of motor cars.

Sitting among the packages, Katie looked up from *Rebecca of Sunnybrook Farm.* "Aunt Helen, you want me to read a book about a girl who lives on a farm, but you don't want me talking about the one I was raised on?"

"Ironic, isn't it?"

"I've heard that word, but I don't know what it means."

"More airs," commented Eugene, turning over the engine. He stuck his arm out the window and steered into the stream of motor cars and clanging trolleys.

"Irony is when you understand the absurdity between an event and the expected result of such an event. In other words, we are recommending you read a book about a girl who goes to live on a farm, but we are forbidding you to speak of your own past."

"Is my past something to be ashamed of?"

"Not at all, Catherine, but children can be cruel. We're trying to prevent the world from being cruel to you."

"The world has already been cruel to me."

Helen nodded. "Excessively so."

Katie opened the book and began to read, and Helen looked up the street. She was always surprised at the new additions, especially the new stores opening on Main Street.

Eugene hooked his arm out the window, signaling a right turn, then headed in the direction of Christ Church. You had to be careful when driving in Greenville. There were no traffic lights.

Katie had another question. "Aunt Helen, do you realize this is a story about a girl sent to live with her aunts."

"Yes," said Helen, smiling. "Perhaps we can learn a thing or two from each other."

Nineteen

Margaret and Mary Kate had just finished putting away their order from Bull's Market when Helen and Katie returned from making their calls.

Helen handed a book to Mary Kate. "I do believe this is yours." It was Charlotte Perkins Gilman's *Concerning Children,* in which the feminist author argued that children should be encouraged to think, rather than obey.

"Indeed it is," said Mary Kate, grinning. "Thank you."

Helen began removing the pins from her hat, and moments later, Katie came through the door wearing her new outfit and carrying a stack of books she needed both arms to hold.

"Nice outfit," commented Margaret.

Helen put down her hat and adjusted her glasses. Now, it was her turn to grin. "You should've seen their faces. I could see each mother trying to understand why such an attractive girl would be fighting with boys, much less the ridiculous accusation that she had beat up her son. They had to wonder if the headmaster had related the story correctly. Perhaps their boys had been fighting *over* this marvelous girl."

Brimming over with enthusiasm, Helen gestured at the transformed girl. "By the way, since she's beginning to show, I purchased two BBs for her."

"Have you ever worn a brassiere?" asked Mary Kate.

Katie thumped the books on the other end of the kitchen table. She straightened up and moved her shoulders around. "Well, I'm not someone who needs all that support."

"Not yet, you don't." Helen gestured at the stack of books. "Took her by Neblett on the way home."

The sisters examined the spines of the books that had been chosen: *Wind in the Willows, The Secret Garden, David Copperfield, Peter Pan, Alice's Adventures in Wonderland, Anne of Green Gables, Uncle Remus,* and *Everyday Etiquette.*

Before the sisters could question Katie about why she had chosen each book, Victoria Lee entered the kitchen.

"Yes, Miss Belle?" she said to Helen. "Catherine said you wished to see me."

Helen stood on the near side of the table; Margaret and Mary Kate sat on stools on the far side. Katie returned to *Rebecca of Sunnybrook Farm* and was soon lost in the story.

"Victoria," said Helen, "it would appear this household needs your assistance."

Victoria glanced at Catherine and nodded approvingly

of her outfit. "Of course. Anything I can do."

"You're aware of Catherine's ride with the veterans yesterday."

"Well . . ." Victoria cleared her throat. "Of course."

"Totally unsuitable for a young lady, I'm sure you agree."

"Miss Belle, it's not my place—"

"No one who lives in this house can fail to notice how well-bred Betty Jean is, and this is from constant effort on your part."

"It must be difficult to maintain such high personal standards in a boarding house," said Margaret.

A flustered Victoria didn't know what to say, other than to thank the ladies for their compliments.

"Catherine grew up in a family that made a great fuss over the war and its veterans."

Amen to that, thought Victoria. She was constantly aware of being among people who did not understand that the war was over. And that the South had lost!

"Did you see how she rode that horse?" asked Helen. "Just like a man."

That had been disgraceful, and Victoria had immediately determined that her daughter would have as little to do with Catherine Belle as possible. Unfortunately, since the girls lived under the same roof and there were no other children to play with, Victoria had yet to come up with a reason to separate the two.

"Catherine may be a fine rider," said Helen, "and believe me, before the war, I saw many a young woman who could ride—"

"You were the best!" This from Margaret.

Helen ignored the compliment. "But riding like a man is completely irrelevant to a woman of good breeding, and though we run a boarding house, it is not the way we were raised."

"So," asked Mary Kate, "could you give Catherine a few hints about being a lady?"

Margaret added, "Things have changed since we were girls."

Victoria was flabbergasted. This wasn't what she'd expected. She glanced at Catherine with her nose stuck in a book. Other books were stacked on the far end of the table, many her daughter had read.

"For instance," said Mary Kate, "you walk with a marvelous carriage. No one would take you for anyone but a lady."

"But our niece," said Helen, "would just as soon run or skip wherever she goes. It comes from being raised on a farm outside New Orleans."

Victoria nodded. "I have that same problem with Betty Jean."

"Well," said Margaret, "they are children."

"But," said Victoria, venturing an opinion, "soon they'll be young ladies with all the accompanying demands and responsibilities."

"Absolutely!" said Mary Kate.

"Then you'll assist us with Catherine's upbringing?" asked Helen. "I, for one, would like to have that casualness removed from Catherine's stride."

The object of their discussion did not look up but continued to read.

"I'll be happy to pass along what I know," said Victoria. "Perhaps we could start with a book. I could have Catherine and Betty Jean walk up and down the upstairs hallway with books on their heads. That shouldn't disturb the boarders."

"They still do that?" asked Helen.

"Of course," said Victoria, feeling at last on sound footing.

Margaret smiled again. "And I thought my sisters were so mean to make me walk around the house with a book on my head. What was the name of that book?"

"The Rules of Decorum," said both sisters.

"Would you be able to give Katie an hour each day?" asked Mary Kate. "Perhaps more on Saturdays?"

Victoria knew the answer to that. If it had not been for the support of these three women, she and her daughter would be out on the street. "Without a doubt. When do you wish me to begin?"

"I'm not sure we can wait," said Helen. "This fight at school is quite worrisome."

"I'll begin immediately. But first I want to speak to Betty Jean and set the proper tone."

"That would be good," said Mary Kate. "Friends do so love doing activities together."

"I'll prepare a syllabus for your approval."

"Grand!" said Margaret, almost shouting.

"Suffrage and temperance meetings?" asked Victoria before going.

"Of course," said Mary Kate.

The other two sisters nodded emphatically.

"And," said Helen, knowing Victoria sewed all her own clothing, "the next time you open your sewing basket, please give Catherine the benefit of your expertise."

"If I might ask, what was Catherine's punishment for

fighting," asked Victoria. "I don't want to be working at cross purposes."

"She had to accompany me to the home of both boys and apologize to, not only the boys, but also their families."

"Good, good," said Victoria, thinking that wasn't nearly enough for such a high-spirited girl. There should be something ongoing. Or final. Like a session with a belt.

"Perhaps you think we should've have taken the strap to her," said Mary Kate.

"Oh, no," said Victoria. "It's not my place."

"There *was* more," said Helen. "Catherine had to convince the mothers, and the headmaster, that she had taken advantage of the boys when they tripped and fell; otherwise, she would not have been able to straddle their backs and pummel the boys."

"I heard that. Not the part about the boys tripping and falling, but that Catherine had them both on the ground and repeatedly struck them."

"Smacking them with her fists is what she told me," said Mary Kate, observing the new bookworm in the family.

"Horrifying!"

"But," added Mary Kate, with some degree of glee, "rather admirable for a girl."

Twenty

Betty Jean had no idea what a pill Katie Belle would turn out to be, especially after Katie rode with those Confederates and beat up two eighth-grade boys. Not to mention Katie woke up screaming every night, something about falling and falling . . .

The girl had serious nightmares. So Betty Jean was ready for Saturday morning, and though she and Katie both had chores, all Betty Jean had to do was charm Margaret Belle, the nicest of the three old maids, for an opportunity to show Katie around Greenville.

Their first stop was the Ottaray Hotel, a five-story brick structure on Main Street and catty-corner to the Confederate monument in the middle of the intersection of Main and College. Situated at the highest point in Greenville, "Ottaray" meant "top of the hill" in Cherokee. The ground floor had huge glass windows sheltered by striped awnings and a veranda on the first, second, and fifth floors.

At the Ottaray, the concierge welcomed Betty Jean

and her new friend with a shiny new dime. The girls rocked back and forth in chairs on the second-story veranda and watched their schoolmates go by in Packards, Whippets, Marlins, and Model Ts. Main Street was paved, as were all intersecting streets, and the one millionth Ford had just rolled off the assembly line.

From the Ottaray, the two girls sauntered down Main Street with its diagonally-parked cars, two lanes of automobile traffic, and trolley cars running down the middle. Overhead ran spaghetti-like wiring for telephones, trolley cars, electricity, and even stock tickers. The girls checked out the latest fashions in Effird's, trying on one hat, then another, and were flipped yet another dime by the department manager. They spent a considerable amount of time in Kress Department Store, where Betty Jean shoplifted some hairpins; they admired shoes in the windows of Patton, Tilman & Bruce, and at Doster Brothers were given a pack of Wrigley's new Doublemint Gum.

Going out the door of the drugstore, the two girls collided with a man wearing a cowboy hat with a snakehead on the front. The pack of gum fell from Betty Jean's hand and she squealed when the man stooped down to pick it up. Katie backed into the drugstore. She was afraid, but not from any snake.

Betty Jean took the gum reflexively. She only had eyes for the snakehead, momentarily at eye level.

The man took off the hat and held it where Betty Jean could see. "It's dead, honey. You've got nothing to worry about." He turned to Katie. "You see . . ." His voice drifted off. "Who are you, girl? Do I know you?"

Katie had slunk back into the drugstore. She knew this man. He had often traded barbs with her father.

Betty Jean cleared her throat. "Catherine Belle. Her aunts own Belles Lodging . . . where we live."

Examining the girl cowering just inside the doorway, Cleve said, "I know the Old Maids' Club, but I don't remember you."

"New Orleans," Katie finally got out. "I'm Catherine Belle from New Orleans, Louisiana."

"What you doing up here? Visiting?"

"My . . . my family . . ." The words would not come.

"Her family died during the hurricane," said Betty Jean from behind the man.

A shadow crossed Cleve and he looked up. A man in a blue suit stood in the doorway. The second man wore a straw boater with matching blue ribbon around the crown.

"Terrorizing children now, are you, Laughlin?"

Cleve got to his feet and placed his cowboy hat on his head. "You cross my property again, Young, and you'll learn who's afraid of who."

The man jutted out his chin. "I can go anywhere I wish. I work for the government. I want to come on your property, Laughlin, I'm coming."

"Yeah, well, you revenuers have always had trouble around Glassy Mountain, and most of us sided with you during the war." He remembered the two girls and motioned them out the door. "You girls get along now."

The girls did, and rather quickly, too.

"Who was that?" asked Katie. "I don't mean the man wearing the cowboy hat. I mean the one in the straw hat."

Betty Jean turned to Katie as they hurried in the direction of the Mansion House. "You mean Agent Young?"

They stopped at the curb where a young woman handed them a broadsheet promoting women's right to vote. "It's your future we're working for, girls."

In the street, a policeman standing under an umbrella stand stopped traffic and motioned them to cross the street.

Katie followed Betty Jean. "Young's a government man?" she asked.

"He goes into the Dark Corner and smashes stills."

Katie realized she should ask what the "Dark Corner" was and did.

"Northeastern corner of Greenville County. Some really rough people live there."

Before she realized it, Katie had agreed.

Her new friend appeared to have a follow-up question but was interrupted when the trolley car rang its bell. They turned around, facing the direction they had just come.

"Let's take the trolley across the river," suggested Betty Jean.

Her friend balked. "The river?"

"Sure. West End's on the other side of the Reedy." The trolley ran a loop around the city, connecting the Textile Crescent on the western side of town to downtown Greenville.

The two girls climbed aboard. Adults paid a nickel, children rode for free. Crossing the new concrete bridge, passengers could see where factories had crowded out the grasses that had once grown in abundance along the water. Katie buried her face in her hands until Betty Jean assured her the river was well behind them.

The trolley passed some rather extravagant homes along Augusta Street, complete with gingerbread trimming, wraparound porches, and even a few strutting peacocks.

"You have no horses," commented Katie.

"Nobody has horses in Greenville. We're very up-to-date." Betty Jean pointed out a house. "That's my favorite. It's William Wilkins' home. Built in French Second Empire style."

Katie didn't know what that meant. She didn't realize she was looking at a double-pitched hip roof, the signature of French architect François Mansart. All she saw was a beautiful home set off the street and heard Betty Jean saying, "When I get married, I'm going to live on this street with a Furman boy."

What could she say to that? No one in Greenville would want to marry a poor girl like her. Then Katie remembered she was no longer poor, but a member of a prominent South Carolina family. She straightened up and looked for the house *she* might wish to live in when she got married.

Betty Jean knocked on several doors and was given a dime or a nickel for a couple of errands run. One took the girls up University Ridge to Furman University, where Betty Jean brazenly flirted with the college boys, lied about their ages, and showed Katie the Florentine-style bell tower that had chimed after every Southern victory during the Civil War. Another errand involved taking a package to the Greenville and Columbia Railroad Depot.

As they passed the triangular-shaped American Bank at the corner of Pendleton and Augusta, a gang of Oaklawn students recognized them as some of the snobs from Central. Betty Jean grabbed Katie's arm and pulled her around a corner where she threw one of her new dimes in the ticket window of the Branwood Theater and they watched a hilarious new comic in *The Tramp*. His name was Charlie Chaplin.

They ate cheese sandwiches at the grill next door, then headed to Brandon Mill to see where "Shoeless Joe" played before being offered a contract by the Chicago White Sox. Eugene often took Betty Jean to Textile League games where she met the cutest boys.

"Just don't tell the boys at Central," cautioned Betty Jean.

On the way to the ball field, they were again seen by the Oaklawn kids and got into a fierce mud ball fight. When the first mud ball smacked into Katie's back, she whirled around and took the fight to the Oaklawn students, throwing with both hands. Not all her mud balls hit their mark, but soon Katie had the air filled with mud.

The Oaklawn kids broke and ran, and Betty Jean had to drag Katie over to the trolley where Katie's anger turned into fear. On the return trip, the trolley stopped on the bridge for tourists to snap pictures of the Reedy River with their Brownie cameras. For the life of her, Betty Jean could not reconcile the hard throwing mud baller with the girl who trembled when the trolley stopped over Reedy River.

Looking at the splattered mud on their white shirtwaists and wool skirts, Betty Jean frowned, then her face brightened. "I know a colored lady who can help us."

So they sat on the back porch in their drawers while the colored lady scrubbed their blouses and hung them out to dry. Anxious that the afternoon was slipping away, the girls determined to walk their clothes dry, thanked the lady, and headed for the country club.

At Sans Souci, they snagged golf balls until one of the caddies ran them off; the same thing happened on the club's clay tennis courts. Leaving Sans Souci, they sold the golf balls, collected another dime, and caught the trolley downtown.

An elderly man gave up his seat for the two girls.

Betty Jean said, "That boy who ran us off?"

"Yes," said Katie, absentmindedly.

"He's one you beat up at school. Name's Mark."

"Might be."

"I'm glad you're not going to beat up anymore boys."

"Why's that?"

"It'll make it difficult for you to find a boyfriend."

The elderly man gripped the strap and smiled. Oh, to be young and in love.

"I don't need a boyfriend."

"Is that because your old boyfriend died in the hurricane?"

Katie looked at her new friend. She had a crush on James Stuart, and more likely James Stuart considered her a mere child.

No! That's not right! He'd kissed her. James must like her, too.

Still, she must remember to be standoffish when she saw James again. She couldn't be too excited. Everyone would think they were meeting for the very first time.

"I'm . . . I'm too young to have a boyfriend," said Katie, mimicking her mother when boys tried to talk to her at church.

The elderly man cleared his throat. The girls looked up.

"That's the very same thing my wife told me over fifty years ago, but it didn't stop *me* from thinking that *I* was *her* boyfriend."

Dismounting from the trolley, they heard a train whistle and decided to take the trolley out West Washington Street to the Southern Railway Depot—the same depot where Katie had arrived only days earlier. There, she gawked at what she had missed by having arrived after dark: the Romanesque Revival-style station with a tower rivaling the one at Fuman.

As they watched the Crescent pull in, the train huffing and puffing and grinding to a halt, steam blew, as did a whistle. Still, Katie could hear an angry insect buzzing overhead. Looking up, she saw a red biplane following the railroad track south.

"What's that?"

"The future of transportation," joked a passenger. Still, everyone watched the plane pass overhead.

"How do they do that?" asked Katie.

Betty Jean had no idea.

"Magic," volunteered the passenger.

Since arriving in the city, Katie had seen many wondrous things, but this flying machine making the insect noise was certainly the most wondrous of them all.

Betty Jean noticed the time on the station manager's pocket watch, and they hurried home to help prepare an early Saturday dinner for those who wished to go dancing at Cleveland Hall or the Imperial Hotel. A tango craze was sweeping the nation, and the enthusiasm for this new dance had cut into the number of people showing up for the quartet that sang in the Belles' parlor on Saturday nights. Robert Patton had an excellent singing voice and he had formed a group upon hearing one of the Negro quartets perform at the Fairview Stock and Agricultural Show in Possum Kingdom the previous year. Redpath's Chatauqua appeared every May, bringing lectures, new plays, and programs for the children.

"The circus comes to town next week," said Betty Jean from where she laid out table settings in the dining room. "You should like that. They have horses."

On the other side of the table, Katie laid out the cloth napkins. "I'd rather go to the library."

Betty Jean stopped what she was doing. "You'd pick the library over the circus? Now that is downright strange."

"Actually, I'd like to read a book about magic."

But after that one joyous afternoon, Katie began to spend an hour a day with Betty Jean's mother learning how to be a lady and another hour at the sewing table. Lessons in penmanship were given by Robert Patton, who was writing a book about the city of Greenville. Since the courthouse had been a gathering place for over a century, whether log cabin or brick building,

Betty Jean had naturally pointed out the structure being demolished beside the former Mansion House Hotel.

"Why are you writing a book about one building?" asked Katie from the roll-top desk where she practiced her cursive.

"That *was* Greenville's name. First, Pleasantburg, then Greenville Court House, and finally Greenville."

"So, you're writing a book about Greenville?"

"Yes, I am."

"Then why not call it *A History of Greenville?*"

"Er . . . Catherine, before our time expires, perhaps we should practice your multiplication tables, especially the eights and nines."

At the end of a session, Robert spoke to one of the sisters.

"What's the problem?" asked Margaret, concerned.

"Catherine's a quick study. She doesn't belong in sixth grade."

Margaret smiled. "The headmaster at Central makes that determination, not us."

"Well, they're slowing down her development if they don't move her up at least one grade." He paused. "Margaret, do you think Catherine's getting enough sleep?"

"What?"

"She falls asleep in my room while doing her work. She falls asleep right at my desk."

Margaret considered this. More than once she'd found Katie asleep with *Alice's Adventures in Wonderland, The Enchanted Castle,* or *Pollyanna* open on her chest.

When Katie hit Dickens and Twain, she slowed down, but the girl was going through books at a rapid pace. Then, there were the nightmares, and once the rumors spread, the nightmares became the reason why mothers never called on Catherine to watch their children when they went out for the evening.

When the nightmares struck, Margaret would take the girl down the hall to the bathroom, wrap her in a blanket, and sit with her in the empty bathtub until she calmed down and fell asleep. It was there that Helen or Victoria Lee would find them the following morning.

"I'll make sure she gets more sleep, Robert. Thank you for bringing that to my attention."

"Well, the girl reads like she's going blind."

Margaret laughed. "I don't think her family valued education as much as we do in this household."

"Did Catherine tell you she wants to learn shorthand and how to type?"

"Why, no, she didn't."

"She thinks . . . well . . ."

"Yes, Robert?" Margaret encouraged him with a warm smile.

"Catherine believes shorthand and typing will guarantee employment once she finishes school."

"She may be right. Every time I go downtown, there's a new hotel being built. Sooner or later, this lodging house will be obsolete."

Margaret passed this information along after Katie fell asleep with *The Campfire Girls of Roselawn* left open on her chest, which Katie had picked up after devouring *Little Women.*

Helen pushed her glasses up on her nose. "Let me know how she does with Latin and I'll be the first to knock on the headmaster's door and tell him we have a prodigy on our hands."

When Katie had no trouble with Latin, Helen did as she promised and Central moved Katie up to seventh grade. Still, this advancement only confirmed to Betty Jean that Katie Belle was a teacher's pet.

How in the world could you be so interested in books when there were so many cute boys at Central?

After school one afternoon, Margaret sat on a cane-bottom chair under the pecan tree and snapped beans while Katie read aloud "In Battle," a poem published a few weeks before its author, Julian Grenfell, was killed in the new war in Europe. Katie was introduced to the poem by Robert Patton, who gave the impression he wished he'd written such an exemplary poem that would enable its author to be remembered in death.

Margaret saw the tears. "Poets who survived the War Between the States did not hold war in the same high regard as those who did not serve. Sidney Lanier wrote about the wonders of nature after returning from the war."

When that didn't stop the tears, Margaret spoke sharply to Eugene, who was using a hoe to turn over soil in the garden. "Not too deep, Eugene. Helen has a good number of hired men buried in that garden."

Eugene snorted, Katie broke down and laughed, and on the far side of the backyard, sheets flapped on the clothesline.

"You know," said Katie, wiping away the tears, "I

really appreciate the opportunity you've given me."

"Pardon?"

"I sit here and read, and you sit there and work."

"You can give me a hand with this here hoe, if you'd like."

"You are working," said Margaret, ignoring Eugene's wisecrack. "You're reading instead of playing with your new toy."

Katie glanced at the carriage house. "You know, I could be earning some money if I went out with Betty Jean every Saturday."

"How's that?" Margaret snapped another bean and threw away the ends.

"People give her money, even if she doesn't do anything."

"Now, that's my idea of a job," said Eugene.

"At first I didn't understand, but I figured Betty Jean and her mother don't have any way to earn money, and the people of Greenville know it."

"Mrs. Lee works for Southern Bell."

"Five or six hours a week, she does, but she doesn't have a real job, just her charities. With an education, you can make something of yourself."

"That's the plan." Margaret noticed Mrs. Dutton staring at them through the window of the house next door. She waved, and Dutton turned away. "When you came to live with us, Katie, your aunts figured you could do chores, or your education could be your chores. Even if you performed your chores to the best of your ability, you'd be no better off than three old maids—"

"And their hired hand," interrupted Eugene.

"But, Aunt Margaret, I make the beds, keep the

bedroom clean, empty trash, wash dishes . . ."

"If you really did chores, you'd master more recipes, clean more rooms, wash the bed linen—"

"Load the hopper with coal," offered Eugene.

"I'm willing to learn," said Katie to her aunt.

"But we aren't willing to teach you the economies of running a boarding house. We want you to make something of yourself."

Katie considered this while Margaret returned to her beans and Eugene to his hoeing.

After a long while, she said, "If . . . if my parents hadn't died, I wouldn't have had this opportunity."

"Even if that's true, please don't mention it again."

For a while, there was only the sound of snapping beans and the hoe striking the ground, then Katie shrieked.

Margaret sat bolt upright, Eugene almost dropped the hoe, and Katie leapt to her feet. James Stuart was directing his wagon into the backyard, pots, pans, and ladles rattling. The girl raced toward him.

"My Lord," muttered Margaret.

"Let's watch the language," said Eugene, straightening up and laughing.

James jumped down from the driver's box, gave the girl a sideways hug, and walked over to the pecan tree.

"Back in town, are you?" asked Margaret.

James snatched a piece of Johnson grass, stripped it to the stem, and stuck the stem in the corner of his mouth. "Just checking on my gal."

"How long will you be here?" asked Margaret.

"Don't know. There's this Roper fellow wants to talk

to me. He's building a textile mill out on the Saluda River."

"So, you're going into the textile business like everyone else." Left unsaid was that James would be getting out of the gun business.

James looked at Katie. "I needed a good excuse to hang around the Greenville Woman's College."

Katie slapped his arm and the necklace around her neck jumped. She tucked it back inside her dress. "Don't be mean or I'll never take you to another girls' baseball game."

James was rubbing his arm. "Wow! You pack a wallop."

Katie looked up from under her eyebrows. "I have a horse now, James. He's called Devil."

"What? I thought Eugene cleaned up that Simplex bike I found and got running. It had a basket and a bell."

"It's obsolete." Leaning on the hoe, Eugene gestured at Katie. "Her word, not mine."

"Obsolete?" asked James. "You are learning big words."

If there was a limit to what the Belle sisters would do for Katie, James hadn't seen it. It was as if all their pent-up love and affection had been waiting for this orphan to be left on their stoop. What in the world had he started?

"Aunt Mary Kate bought him when the circus came to town."

Greenville had always been a regular stop for the circus. The animals and performers unloaded at the

Augusta Street terminal and paraded through the West End, over the Gower Bridge, and into downtown. All but the elephants. Those animals were required to splash through the shallows of Reedy River, then up Main Street. Negroes cooked fish, wrapped it in bread, and made more money in a few days than they did all year, and before one of the performances, Katie made sure Aunt Mary Kate discovered the horse she'd fallen in love with. Katie had noticed the animal while she and Betty Jean watched the circus march into town.

"Can't afford him," said the horse's owner to Mary Kate. "He eats too much, and I don't have time to train him. Give you a good price."

"And what would that be?" asked Mary Kate.

"Four dollars. Price of motor cars is driving down the price of horseflesh."

"Not to mention the animal's name."

In the carriage house behind Belles Lodging, a reddish-brown horse kicked up his heels when the doors were swung open.

"My Lord," said James, "it's a mustang!"

"Please, James," said Margaret. "Your language."

Katie looked from her aunt to the salesman. "That means he's a good one?"

"It means someone has to break him in." James turned to the door where Margaret and Eugene stood. "You can't allow Katie to ride this animal until he's been properly broken in."

"And who would do that, James?" asked Margaret with a warm smile.

A few days later, Katie was sitting at the preparation table reading while Mary Kate churned milk to make butter. Not far from her reach was a pack of Hershey's kisses.

"You know," said Katie, looking up from her book, "some of the stories I read are in the Bible, too."

"Well, child, there aren't that many plots."

"What's a plot?"

"The storyline. They haven't covered that in seventh grade?"

Katie shook her head.

"Plot is the main story of the book. You've read *Peter Rabbit,* haven't you?"

Katie nodded.

"What's the main story of *Peter Rabbit?*"

Katie thought for a moment. "What happens to Peter once he goes under McGregor's fence."

Mary Kate stopped churning long enough to unwrap a Hershey's kiss. Several pieces of tinfoil lay near other kisses that hadn't been unwrapped. "All that happens makes up the plot."

Katie considered this. "Aunt Mary Kate, do you think I'll ever write a story?"

"I didn't know you were interested."

"I don't think I was until Mr. Patton explained that stories were written by people."

Mary Kate smiled. Kids could say the darnedest things. She popped the chocolate into her mouth.

"It might be fun to write a story."

The old woman returned to her churning. "I don't think writers believe it's fun, but hard work."

"If I had an idea, I could write a story, couldn't I?"

"Of course. What kind of story were you interested in?"

"I could write about growing up in the Dark Corner."

"Well, if you do, don't let anyone read it but your aunts."

"Not even Mr. Patton?"

Remembering how Robert's mouth had gotten him in trouble at the dinner table last week, arguing over literacy requirements for immigrants, Mary Kate said, "Especially Mr. Patton."

There was a long silence, broken only by the sound of the churn; then Katie asked, "Aunt Mary Kate, may I ask you something kind of personal?"

"Of course, child. What is it?"

Katie closed the book and stared into her lap. "You remember that day when we were out riding in your car and Aunt Helen told me the story of the three sisters who moved from Blind Switch into Greenville but never married?"

"Yes?" The churning slowed.

"Well, Margaret was only ten years old. Why didn't Margaret get married after she grew up?"

The churning stopped. "Margaret sometimes embraces her ideals too passionately."

Kate looked up. "That's the reason I'm here."

"True, and as you've learned in the short time you've been living here, there's no one more loyal than Margaret."

"Are you saying Aunt Margaret didn't marry because she wanted to be loyal to you and Helen?"

"Your words, child, not mine."

Twenty-one

George Roper was a banker whose roots went all the way back to the founding of Charles Town. His ancestors had sailed with the pirate, James Stuart, and their two families had been entwined for the last hundred years. While Stuart ships continued to ply the North Atlantic, the Roper family moved into merchandising and finally investment banking.

When the Civil War ended, Roper and Sons had a good bit of money in the Bahamas and the Stuarts were bankrupt. Still, this did not mean the Ropers moved ahead of the Stuarts. When the Ropers were finally able to transfer their money back to this country, they became tentative. Charleston had become an economic backwater, not the powerhouse it had been before the war. While the Stuarts moved boldly, having little to lose, Roper and Sons allowed questions to dog them for decades.

When would Reconstruction end?

How long would the Negro remain in power?

Would the white man become involved in politics again?

If the white man did become active again, did that mean the Yankees would return?

The federal income tax had come and gone, but national panics were a curse on a prostrate South. So while the Stuarts boldly rebuilt their fortune, the Ropers sat on their assets until Yankee money began to flow into South Carolina in the form of textile machinery from New England.

That caught the attention of a thirty-six-year-old widower working for Roper and Sons. George had attended the Citadel on scholarship, then had his business fail during the Panic of '07, so when his cousins offered him a job as a bookkeeper, he grabbed the opportunity. From the first day on the job, George watched his cousins turn down those from the upstate who came to Charleston looking for money to build textile mills. The last group to be rejected—this one from Spartanburg—cursed George's cousins for their bullheadedness.

"If Yankees can sell the machinery for the mills, how long before they realize they can own the buildings housing that machinery and scoop off all the profits? It's no accident the first textile mill in Grantville was built by a Pennsylvania Yankee."

This made sense to George, and he set out to convince the family that Roper and Sons should invest in textiles. But the same reluctance that held George hostage to his job held Roper and Sons hostage to their assets.

"We must consider the widows and orphans who depend on this bank for their monthly allowance," was the unanimous opinion of the senior members of the firm. "You, of all people, George, a widower with two small children, should understand this."

The reaction of the board to his proposal caused George to fall into a funk. A similar bout of melancholy had claimed him when his young wife had died from yellow fever.

"Why don't you purchase a carriage?" asked his mother-in-law, who had moved in to care for her motherless grandchildren. "You could sell subscriptions for your own mill."

"I've never needed a carriage living in Charleston. I walk everywhere I go."

His mother-in-law became more straightforward. "Perhaps it's time to move to the upcountry, George. You've lost a wife to yellow fever and I've lost a daughter and a husband."

That finally reached George, a proud Charlestonian. "You'd leave home?"

"Only if you build this cotton mill you talk about incessantly. They don't have diseases in the upcountry like we do in the low country. I remember vacationing at Chick Springs in Taylors, before our family lost all its money in the Panic of 'seventy-three. The weather there was marvelous."

"What would you do while I'm gone, Mother?"

"Don't worry about us, George. Leave the children with me, buy a carriage, and travel the upstate in search for subscriptions."

"Roper and Sons won't back me."

"If you're accepting subscriptions for a new mill, why wouldn't people naturally believe the mill is being built by your family?"

"You mean lie to people?"

"No, George, just don't tell them everything. Move with that old confidence and swagger you once had when you courted Henrietta. My husband and I were completely taken in. We thought you were one of the partners at Roper and Sons."

"That was a different situation. I didn't have children."

"Then find another girl, George. Your children need a mother, not a grandmother."

The upcountry was so different from the low country that George became invigorated, not to mention that if a Roper asked for money, people lined up to subscribe. As did fellow graduates of the Citadel. After all, Roper and Sons was one of the investment houses the state went to to float bond issues. So George purchased a yellow Stutz Bearcat and had it delivered to Greenville, and anywhere he went, the yellow car drew a crowd. In short order, the land was purchased, the mill built, and a village of workers was assembled. Looms were ordered from an outfit in New England.

Greenville's business culture was one of building on the shoulders of previous generations. After Vardry McBee saw the potential of a trading post astride the wagon road from Augusta to western North Carolina and eastern Tennessee, Benjamin Perry brought South Carolina back into the Union by preaching the gospel of hard work, industralization, and the value of Yankee money; he was joined by Captain Ellison Adger Smyth, who, with no experience in textiles, became a specialist in organizing mills and banks. Those giants were followed by Lewis Parker, who arrived from Abbeville to practice law, but instead went into the textile business and ended up controlling more than a million spindles; John T. Woodside, whose family created the Woodside empire, and along the way became the richest man in the upstate; and J. E. Sirrine, who built just about every significant building in the upstate. Like George, few of these men were originally from Greenville, but all were dedicated to the "Pearl of the Piedmont."

Roper found himself swept up in the current generation's enthusiasm for improving their lot: Alester Furman, Harry J. Haynsworth, both Sirrines, and the Parker Brothers. And what did these people know about George when he first arrived?

All they needed to know was whether he wanted to make Greenville grow. Roper did, and was immediately granted membership in the Chamber of Commerce, the Rotary Club, the Sans Souci Country Club, and the Poinsett Club. George was already a Master Mason and an Odd Fellow.

Moving to Greenville became a life-changing event, as was the day when the cars of the Southern Railway jumped the track and people swarmed out of the woods to pick over the wreckage. Since no one from the Dark Corner had any use for textile machinery, James Stuart went into the foothills north of Greenville and hired teamsters—at least, those who weren't still celebrating from picking over the wreckage. Soon, the flatcars were back on track and the looms moving to the mill on the Saluda River. But an odd thing happened to George while overseeing the recovery.

George tapped James on the shoulder and pointed to a figure on horseback, a dark-haired young woman at the edge of the forest. She appeared to be dressed completely in white and wore bloomers.

"Who's that?" asked George.

"I don't know," said James, suddenly angry. He recognized the mustang.

"We call her Bloomer Babe," volunteered Earl Laughlin. "She rides through the Dark Corner just like a man."

James shot the teamster a hard look. Overhead, a bright yellow biplane followed the track south. At the sound of the plane's engine everyone looked up, including the Bloomer Babe.

Returning his attention to the rider at the edge of the woods, George said, "Nice-looking woman, and bold enough to ride alone. I'd like to meet her. Which one of you men has the fastest horse?" George had ridden to the crash site in James's wagon, pots and pans clattering in his ear. "I'll give that man a ten-dollar gold piece for the fastest horse."

The offer of a ten-dollar gold piece made all their horses fast.

"Which one, James?"

Stuart pointed at the stallion about to be mounted by Cleve Laughlin. "His."

"What? Hey, Stuart, that's not right."

Still, Laughlin said make it twenty dollars and the horse was Roper's for the day. George flipped a gold coin to Laughlin, mounted up, and crossed the grading, disappearing into the forest.

While George was gone, Cleve and Earl got into it. The argument began when Earl told his cousin he was sick and tired of making ends meet sharecropping and not having anything left over at the end of the day, week, or year. No cash money meant he couldn't buy anything extra for his family, and jobs like this one didn't come along often enough. Earl was considering moving his family into the mill village being built by George Roper.

"That's just plain stupid." Cleve gestured at the forest on the other side of the railroad tracks. "You're free to live how you want out here. You go to work for Roper and he tells you what to do."

Earl gestured at his cousin's pants' pocket. "Seems like he pays pretty well."

"That's a one-time deal. You go to work in the mill and you work from daylight to dusk."

"I already work daylight to dusk. I work every day, including Sundays. In the mill villages, they got schools, churches, and you end up with money in an envelope at the end of the week. Isn't that right, Stuart?"

The Charlestonian nodded. "They also train you to operate the looms. Your family can work there. Wives, kids, everybody."

"Oh, don't listen to him," said Cleve. "Stuart works for Roper. As far as schools and churches go, Mountain Hill School is doing just fine."

Earl shook his head. "I don't know. Those mill village schools sound pretty good to me."

"You know the Baileys and the Phillips—they came back to Glassy, tails tucked between their legs."

"Aw, neither of them has any patience. You see them

at church. They fidget all the time. And the whiskey they bring to market—"

At that remark, more mouths than Cleve's told Earl Laughlin to shut up.

James laughed. "Like I don't know where moonshine comes from. Some of you people pay in moonshine, and you sure as the devil buy a lot of sugar."

"Uh-huh," said Earl, grinning. "Ole Stuart knows how to make a buck. He puts our 'shine on a Greenville and Columbia railway car and ships it to Charleston. People in Charleston love their liquor."

"Another reason to stay here and raise more corn."

George returned a couple of hours later, confessing that the girl wearing the white bloomers had immediately lost him, and he had spent the rest of the time trying to find his way out of the woods.

"By the way, Laughlin," said George, returning Cleve's horse, "I had to fire at a couple of your fellows in there. They tried to take the horse, and that wouldn't do."

Everyone stared at George. No one was sure if Roper was serious or not. Turned out, George wasn't kidding. One man was dead, another severely injured, and the dead man's son now had unfinished business with George Roper.

James had his own problem. George would keep after the so-called Bloomer Babe until he caught her. Figuring the only way to end this charade was to introduce George to Katie, he did just that over Sunday dinner at Belles Lodging, where James had taken a room while working for Roper and Sons.

Katie and Betty Jean chattered like schoolgirls, which was exactly what they were. Having children at the table, thought James, must've made George feel right at home—that is, once George got over the shock of Katie being the Bloomer Babe.

"Er . . . Catherine," asked George, "do you ride often?"

"Oh, yes, sir," she said from the other side of the table. "I have a horse. His name's Devil. I ride him all over the county."

"When she isn't studying Latin," groused Betty Jean.

Katie blushed and looked into her lap.

"Ever ride through the Dark Corner?"

"She's forbidden to ride there," said Helen Belle, speaking for the sisters. Sunday dinner was the only meal all three sisters shared with their guests.

Katie looked pleadingly at James Stuart.

"Yes," said James, smiling. "She's one hell of a horsewoman."

All the women shushed him and told him to watch his language.

"Sorry, sorry," said James.

Katie nodded in gratitude.

Robert Patton took this opportunity to regale George with tales of how quickly Catherine was advancing through her grades. At Central they were talking about moving her up to eighth grade.

"I'm already in eighth grade," said Betty Jean, proudly.

Roper looked from Catherine to his foreman.

James only smiled.

After dinner, James, George, and Robert took their cigars to the rockers on the front porch.

"You just saved me from one huge embarassment, James," said George, sitting down.

"Well, you do have to do business in this town."

"The other lady at the table," inquired George, puffing on his cigar. "Mrs. Lee?"

Robert jumped into the conversation and filled George in about Victoria's sad tale, then the book he was writing about Greenville Courthouse.

"A whole book about one building?" asked George.

Thereupon, Robert gave George a dose of Greenville history and how folks from the low country had been vacationing in the upcountry for years. Even Joel Poinsett, known for the red-leafed plant he brought back from Mexico while serving there as ambassador.

"In the upcountry Poinsett is primarily known as the builder of a Gothic-style arched bridge," said Robert, "the oldest in the state. As president of the state Board of Public Works, Poinsett supervised the building of the road through the Saluda Gap, causing Greenville to have more in common with Knoxville, Tennessee, than Charleston, South Carolina."

Poinsett, a rice planter, lived in Greenville during the summer and built a home and gardens on White Horse Road. An ardent Unionist, he repeatedly clashed with John C. Calhoun, but by the end of the two men's lives, it would be James C. Furman, president of the school named for his father, who would lead Greenville into seceding from the Union. Furman was passionate about slaveholders' rights, and when it came to women, he was just as passionate: Women should go along to get along.

Robert left the porch to take a phone call from one of his cohorts concerning the new superintendent of education, J. L. Mann, who had demanded that Greenville school district provide free textbooks for every student.

"Nobody takes care of books they've been given," said Robert to his friend on the other end of the line. "For books to be treasured, they must be purchased by the students themselves, or their parents."

The front door had been left open, and George rose from his rocker and closed the door, shutting off the one-sided conversation from the foyer.

Seated again, George asked James, "Would you be able to locate Mrs. Lee's husband?"

"I thought I was to coordinate the Greenville office with the one at the mill, and the railroads with both offices."

"If you can't find Lee, I'm sure the Pinkertons can find him."

Now James turned to him. "George, most people think of the Pinkertons as strikebreakers."

Another drag off his cigar. "Where would you start?"

James considered this. "Betty Jean has a crush on me. If her father's in town, she'll tell me."

"I would've thought it would be Catherine. She looks up to you. Anyone can see that."

"She's almost six years younger than I am, George."

Roper shrugged. "I was eight years older than my wife."

"And Henrietta was nineteen when you married her. Those two girls are only fourteen."

"You certainly took that job I offered you quick enough."

"I'm only in Greenville to keep an eye on my subscription."

"Yes, yes. Of course you are."

The next time Victoria, Betty Jean, and the Old Maids' Club attended a women's suffrage meeting, Katie chose not to accompany them. The Belle sisters went as a group, huddling with their friends from the Thursday Club: Frances Perry Beattie, Martha Orr Patterson, and Mary Putnam Gridley, the first woman in the South to run a textile mill. Betty Jean only attended meetings because her mother allowed her to walk over to the Woman's College and swim in the pool on Tuesday and Friday afternoons.

Katie spent that evening in Robert Patton's room working on her studies. She'd already figured out how to survive at Central: memorization, drills, and practice; all preparation for arithmetic matches on the blackboards and those humiliating spelling bees. And though she couldn't sing a lick anymore than James Stuart, she'd signed up for the spring musical. Katie also learned she enjoyed the Virginia reel and was actually looking forward to coming out at cotillion.

But before they got down to her studies, Katie had to listen to another lecture from Robert Patton, this one concerning women's wear, another leftover from the dinner conversation.

"The woman's dress is narrowing, becoming shorter, and the corset's longer. The fashion seems to compress the hips so women will finally discard the skirt and wear bloomers."

Her aunts would've been horrified at a man speaking so boldly to a member of the opposite sex, especially a young girl, but with Katie, this lecture went in one ear and out the other. She already wore bloomers—when she rode like a man.

It had been difficult to come by a saddle that was the proper fit, but Katie insisted Devil may as well be sold if she had to ride sidesaddle. The old maids never called her bluff, so Katie turned over the problem of finding a saddle to James Stuart. James could find anything if given enough time.

When the suffrage meeting concluded at the new YMCA on East Coffee Street, the women left as a group, walking to the trolley stop on Main.

"Victoria," hissed a bearded figure from the shadows.

"Uncle Johnny" Holmes was just beginning what would become a long career at the Greenville YMCA and he regularly escorted the suffragists to the trolley stop. When he noticed that Victoria and Betty Jean were not with the group, he quickly returned to the door where he saw a bearded man wrapping his arms around the child.

Over the girl's head, the stranger said, "If you don't mind, I wish to speak to my family alone."

"Mrs. Lee?" asked Uncle Johnny.

"Everything's fine. It's been a long time since my daughter's seen her father. He travels a great deal."

"Yes, ma'am." And Uncle Johnny returned to the trolley stop. He had not lived in Greenville when Edmund Lee had absconded with people's funds.

"Father," begged Betty Jean, "will you come home with us?"

Edmund Lee looked over the girl's head to his wife. "That depends on your mother."

Betty Jean turned to her mother. "Oh, do invite him, Mother. Father can sleep with you and I can sleep on a pallet like Katie."

"What can I do for you, Edmund?" His wife had yet to embrace him.

"It's good to see you, too, Victoria." He glanced at the entrance to the YMCA. "I figured I'd find you here."

"Betty Jean and I have few opportunities to go out at night."

"Father, if you came home to live with us, we could go to the Bijou and see the moving pictures."

"I'm not sure your mother cares for my being in Greenville."

"Of course she does. You want Father to come home with us, don't you, Mother?"

"I've told you before, Betty Jean, your father has business that takes him away from Greenville for long periods of time."

"We'll go with him." Betty Jean turned to her father. "Father, can we come along?"

"Where I go is not suitable for ladies, and if there's anything your mother is, it's a lady. What do you hear from your family?" he asked his wife.

"Absolutely nothing."

Betty Jean took her father's hand. "I write them every month, but they must be terribly busy in Ohio."

"Just as you are, Edmund," said his wife, a degree of bitterness finally creeping into her voice.

"I wish there was something I could do, my dear. You must believe me when I say so."

"There is, Father. You can come home with us."

"I'm sorry, Betty Jean, but I have quite a few responsibilities."

Edmund gave the girl another hug. "Now why don't you wait at the trolley stop while I speak to your mother?"

Betty Jean did not wish to go, but her parents insisted. She gave her father another hug, told him how much she liked his new beard, and dawdled on the way to the trolley stop, occasionally turning to look at her parents. Her mother had not hugged her father, and in Betty Jean's mind, that was the source of their estrangement. Hugs could solve just about any problem.

Edmund held out some money. "This is for you and the child. It's only fifty dollars, but it's all I have."

Victoria glanced at the money but did not take it. "What would I do with it? It's not enough to pay all we owe."

"You don't owe anything. They can't hold you responsible." He thrust the money at her again. "Here, take it, if not for you, then for the child."

"Edmund, your daughter is not going to be raised on your ill-gotten gains."

"You weren't so proud when I carried you over the threshold of our new house in Boyce Lawn."

"That was before I understood the depth of your depravity."

"Oh, you are such a prig!" Lee jammed the money into his pocket and glanced at the trolley stop. "I'll bet

Betty Jean would take it. Her spine hasn't ossified as much as yours. I just might give her this money."

"I'll turn you over to the sheriff. You're to stay away from our daughter, Edmund, do you hear?"

He turned on his heel and walked away.

"Do you hear me, Edmund?" said his wife, trailing him into the shadows. "It'll be the county lockup if you get that child's hopes up." When her husband didn't respond, Victoria allowed a few sobs to escape while still in the shadows, then she dabbed at her eyes and joined the other suffragists at the trolley stop.

Betty Jean was too excited to keep such news secret. Upon being told Katie had turned in for the night—the nightmares had diminished with all her reading—Betty Jean related her news to James Stuart as he exited the upstairs bathroom after taking a shower. Drying his hair with a towel, James warned Betty Jean to keep such family business to herself.

Betty Jean seized his free hand and looked up at him. "Why, James," she said, coyly, "I thought you *were* family."

James broke free and told Betty Jean to get to bed. Once in his room on the ground floor, he dressed, left the house, and took the trolley to the West End.

After asking around, he returned to the Ottaray Hotel, where George Roper was staying. "Edmund's at the West End Hotel," he told George. "Probably intends to take the train for Columbia in the morning. Want me to inform the sheriff?"

"I don't see how that helps Betty Jean and her mother. Let me see if I can talk some sense into him."

Twenty-two

Edmund Lee observed a man watching him from the front of the railway car and wondered if he was some kind of law. It wasn't until the train pulled out of the depot that the man came down the aisle and introduced himself.

"George Roper, Mr. Lee. May I join you?"

"I believe you have the wrong man."

George took a clipping from his coat pocket, gave it to Lee, and sat down.

Edmund unfolded the yellowing clipping from the Greenville *Piedmont.* It featured the 1907 story about Lee absconding with several thousand dollars of Greenvillians' money. The article was accompanied by a picture of Lee sans beard.

"You know, Edmund—you don't mind if I call you 'Edmund,' do you? There are a good number of these articles pasted on walls in the homes of people you swindled. They'll never forget you any more than the Negro will forget Abraham Lincoln."

George took a metal case from an inside coat pocket, popped it open, and offered a cigar to Lee. Edmund shook his head and looked out the window at the motor cars traveling along Anderson Road. As usual, several had conked out and drivers had the hoods up working on them.

"I bet we can find one or two people on this train who remember you." George returned the metal case to his pocket and crossed his legs. He bit off the tip of the cigar and spit it on the floor. "I know I remember and I was living in Charleston."

Edmund said nothing. He didn't even look at George.

"What you need to do is never return to South Carolina."

Edmund turned on him. "I have family in Greenville."

"I know," said George, scratching a match on the bottom of his shoe, "and I'd like to purchase them."

Edmund smiled. "I believe they passed an amendment to the Constitution forbidding the buying and selling of people."

"Oh, Edmund," said George, lighting the cigar, "people can still be bought and sold. We just need to determine your price."

Edmund's eyes narrowed. "Divorce is not permitted in the state of South Carolina."

"Oh, Edmund, your wife will not be divorcing you in South Carolina."

George took a drag off his cigar and let out a breath. The lighting of the cigar must've been some sort of signal because two large men came forward from the rear of the passenger car and took seats facing Roper and Lee.

George gestured at a third man occupying a seat across the aisle. "Judge Randall of Atlanta. Judge Randall is willing to grant your wife a divorce as the train passes through Georgia."

"What's in it for you?"

"I plan to marry your wife."

Edmund laughed and sat up. "Oh, you do, do you?"

"I have two children living with my mother-in-law in Charleston. My wife died several years back. I thought Victoria and I might blend our families together."

"Victoria is married. To me."

"Yes, she is, Edmund, and if you don't sign the divorce papers, I can promise that you will go to prison. Do you really want Betty Jean to grow up visiting her father in prison? The people of Greenville have gone out of their way to make your daughter and her mother feel like a part of their community. You can ruin that, too, if you care to, but I don't think you're that selfish."

"I'll need money."

"You will always need money."

"Ten thousand dollars is my price."

"What about one hundred dollars?"

Edmund laughed. "You must be kidding."

"One hundred dollars a week for as long as you remain out of South Carolina."

"A hundred a week?"

"Think of it as an annuity."

"For how long?"

"Like I said, as long as you can stay away."

"Where will the money be sent?"

"You tell me." George took out a checkbook and his fountain pen. He unscrewed the cap.

"A hundred dollars is not enough to get started elsewhere."

"There's a sweetener."

"A sweetener? How much?"

George gestured at one of the large men sitting across from them. The man opened his coat for Edmund to see a wad of bills in his inside coat pocket and a pistol strapped to his broad chest. George nodded, and the man took the wad of bills from his pocket and handed them to Lee.

"How much is this?" asked Edmund, sitting up even straighter.

"One thousand dollars—payable upon signing the paperwork allowing your wife to divorce you for desertion."

Edmund stuffed the bills inside his coat. "I want to examine that paperwork."

"And you shall."

George got to his feet and allowed the judge to take the seat next to Edmund. The judge made Lee swear on a Bible that he was who he said he was; then the papers were signed and witnessed by the two large men. Edmund Lee had allowed his wife to divorce him in the presence of a judge and two Pinkerton detectives while the train passed through North Georgia.

A whistle blew and the judge got to his feet, shook hands all around, and moved to the rear of the passenger car. The detectives did not join him.

"The judge and I must get off here," said George, continuing to stand in the aisle, "but you and these two fellows will continue on to Atlanta, then Miami where they'll put you on a ship bound for San Francisco. It leaves day after tomorrow."

"San Francisco?"

George clapped Edmund on the back as the train pulled into the North Georgia railway station. Parked in the lot was a yellow Stutz Bearcat with a young man sitting behind the wheel. "Think of it, Edmund. You'll sail through the Panama Canal. All those locks—I've heard it's quite a thrill."

"But I didn't agree to go to San Francisco."

"No, you didn't, but since it's all-expenses paid, plus another thousand waiting for you in an affiliate bank of Roper and Sons, why wouldn't you?"

"And if I return to South Carolina or write my daughter?"

"The annuity ends and you go to prison faster than you can say Jack Robinson. Going to prison will give you plenty of time to come up with a decent explanation as to why you deserted your family."

Edmund smiled up at George. "You really think my wife's hands were clean in that affair?"

"Hardly. I examined your journals in the Greenville County Courthouse. The records of your company were kept in your wife's handwriting."

"And you're still willing to marry her?"

"Mr. Lee, it's been almost ten years since you abandoned your wife and child. Don't you think they've paid enough for their association with you?"

Edmund laughed. "As long as you keep an eye on your wallet. I intend to collect my hundred dollars for a very long time."

"Oh, I shall. I intend to employ your wife to keep my books. That way she'll know if I'm a decent marital prospect or not."

✣ ✣ ✣

"Miss Jim" Perry, daughter of a professor at the Woman's College and bearing her father's name, arrived at the offices of Southern Bell just as Victoria Lee finished her relief shift. "Miss Jim" was South Carolina's first female attorney, but to accomplish this she'd had to pass the bar in California, where she'd earned her bachelor's degree. She was now on track to become a partner in the Haynsworth law firm, and as a favor to that firm, the manager of Southern Bell was taking a longer than usual lunch.

"Would you have a moment?" asked Perry, gesturing Lee into the manager's office.

Victoria's hand rose to her mouth. "It's Edmund, isn't it?"

"Yes, Mrs. Lee. In Georgia, he signed the proper paperwork allowing you to divorce him for desertion."

"No, no, no!" Victoria's legs weakened. She stumbled over to a chair and sat down, legs splayed. "But he can't do that. I still love him."

Twenty-three

Almost three years later, the efforts and the lies of the Old Maids' Club finally paid off. Their niece, Catherine Belle, was presented at the Greenville Cotillion Club.

Each year, the daughters of the social elite celebrated their coming out with the girls' fathers presenting them in a ceremony fashioned after the debutante balls held in Charleston. Wearing a white gown and long, white gloves, each debutante was introduced to the audience, then walked around the stage, guided by her father. Her younger male escort joined them and escorted the debutante from the stage. For James Stuart, it meant doing double duty.

The Old Maids' Club had no men to perform such a social chore, except for Robert Patton, the author, who accompanied Victoria Lee and presented Betty Jean to proper Greenville society. If rules were being bent for uncles who survived their brothers and if Robert Patton could present Betty Jean, James Stuart, scion of a prominent Charleston family, could present and escort Catherine Belle.

The night of cotillion, James wore a tux, and on his arm, Katie Belle devastated the competition with the latest fashion from Paris, a tangle of black curls falling around her head, and just the right touch of makeup. Her appearance put the boys on notice that Katie Belle was a force to be reckoned with, especially one young man who couldn't take his eyes off her.

It also proved to Allison McKelvey that being a lady trumped all other cards a woman might play, and it didn't hurt that her slender frame had the perfect figure to bridge the gap between the Gibson Girl of the past and the coming age of flappers. From the rear of the ballroom and dressed resplendently, the members of the Old Maids' Club beamed proudly.

James had seen Katie eyeing Mark from the moment the young man's name appeared on her dance card.

"You're not to have anything to do with that young man," ordered James after returning from the obligatory dance with Mark's date. For the first time James realized Katie did not wear her mother's necklace and this incensed him.

Katie was taken aback, but tonight of all nights she must be a lady. "Why, James, whatever do you mean?"

"Mark can be quite charming, but his date is left with her girlfriends, not her escort."

"Yes," said Katie, smiling toward a corner of the ballroom where the couple appeared to be arguing. "Looks like he can't make up his mind."

"Katie, are you trying to start another feud—this one in Greenville? Tom Gower built the first two bridges across the Reedy River and the first trolley car system connecting both train depots. One of his relatives is not someone to cross."

"Feud?" asked Katie, elevating her nose and working her fan. "Really, James, I'm quite sure I don't know what you're talking about."

James shook his head. "Well, Allison, you finally have arrived. I'll get a cup of punch so we can drink to you finding your soul mate so early in life."

"Thank you," she said. "But make sure this one has a bit more punch to it. A bootlegger like you should be able to come up with something special."

James's eyes flashed as he turned away. Katie Belle knew everything but understood nothing.

A few months later, James had another run-in with Mark, this one at a roadhouse in Spartanburg County.

It wasn't his interest in cockfights that drew James to the roadhouse. Being from Charleston, he'd seen a cockfight or two, and though they disgusted him, every once in a while he had to attend one—very much like having to drink moonshine with his customers. He did business with these people.

Cotton had never been "King" in the upstate. The money was in corn, but when prices fell, farmers found a better use for their corn. They turned it into moonshine and sold it to roadhouses, quite a feat in a "dry" county. It was at one of those roadhouses that the deputy sheriff found James Stuart playing poker one night with several customers and a couple of soldiers from Camp Sevier.

"Read 'em and weep," said James, laying his cards

across the table where the last of the soldiers' money lay.

Most of the boys threw in their cards and called it a night. All but one soldier, a tall, narrow-faced kid who dropped his cards on the table and accused James of cheating.

James laughed at him. "Mark, you're no good at cards. Stick to what you do best. Girls seem to like you."

Mark scrambled to his feet and pulled back his jacket, revealing a small pistol strapped to the belt of his military uniform.

"And I say you were cheating," said Mark, swaying back and forth.

His friends tried to reason with him, saying that he should forget the money, that they had little use for money where they were headed.

The deputy appeared from the smoky haze. "You boys need to get back to Greenville County before you get into trouble."

Mark gestured at James, who sat across the table, hands in his lap. On James's hip rested the Webley automatic pistol.

"He's got my money," said Mark, continuing to sway.

Another player, one wearing a cowboy hat with a snakehead on the front, looked up. "He got my money, too, kid, but you don't hear me whining."

Mark shifted around to eye this new threat. A couple of women broke away from their dates and wandered over to the table. This was just the sort of thing that wound their stems.

"Go home, Mark," said James. "I don't want to fight you."

"You shouldn't have cheated. I have every right to shoot you down where you stand."

"Mark," said James, drawing his feet under him, "that's the liquor talking. I'm not standing. I'm sitting down, but you're too drunk to notice."

"You're too drunk to recognize what happened," said Cleve Laughlin. "Stuart just had a run of luck like he never had before."

James protested this characterization while the deputy reminded Mark what county he was in. "Your grandpa might've once been governor, but if you're going to do any killing, you'd better take it across the county line where your friends are."

"Yeah," encouraged one of Mark's buddy, a dandy wearing a straw boater. "Wait until Stuart comes back to Greenville and shoot him there." He got to his feet.

"I can take him here. Now."

"Mark," asked the deputy, "you know what kind of pistol that is? Stuart's weapon can spit out bullets like a Gatling gun."

Mark turned his head but had difficulty focusing on the angular man. "I know his weapon. I tried to buy it off him once."

"And I sold you the one you're wearing," said James, still seated at the table. "It's no Webley."

"And since you last haggled with him," said the deputy, "he's begun carrying the Webley in a spring-loaded holster. That pistol fairly leaps into his hand."

"I can still take him."

"Then make your move," said James, tired of all this talk.

The soldier fumbled for his pistol, trying to remove the weapon from its small holster. Over muttered curses came the screeching of chairs, some falling to the floor. Men and women backed away.

By the time Mark got his weapon out, James had leaned across the table, reversed the Webley, and clubbed Mark up side the head. A look of surprise appeared on the young man's face. He dropped his pistol and slumped back into his chair.

His friend, the dandy wearing the straw boater, said, "Hey, that's no fair." And he reached for his own pistol.

The deputy stuck a finger in the young man's back. With his other hand, he knocked the straw hat off the young man's head. "Drop it! Drop it right now!"

The young man did.

Another of Mark's soldier friends stood up, dumping a woman from his lap. The woman landed with a thud and a yelp.

"What's going on here?" The soldier had no pistol, but he did carry a switchblade. He brought the knife out of his pocket and flicked it open.

Cleve Laughlin removed his cowboy hat and swatted the blade downward. The young man cursed and turned on him, but before he could bring up the knife, Cleve extended a leg and connected with the young man's knee.

The soldier yelped, dropped his blade, and grabbed his knee. Cleve slid to the edge of his chair and kicked the knife across the room, where it disappeared in the crowd.

"Okay," said the deputy, retrieving the straw hat and

its owner's pistol from the floor. "Time for you boys to head back to Greenville County."

Mark's friend realized he'd been disarmed by an unarmed deputy. "Hey, that's not fair!" he said again.

Cleve picked up Mark's pistol and handed it to the deputy.

Motioning to the unconscious Mark, the deputy said, "And take him with you." The deputy emptied the rounds from Mark's pistol on the table followed by the rounds from the dandy's pistol.

Mark's friends grabbed him under the arms and hauled him to his feet. Blood ran down the side of his head. The Spartanburg boys liked that. They hooted the Greenville boys from the room and out of the roadhouse. Catcalls followed them all the way to a Cadillac where Mark was dumped into the backseat along with both pistols.

"Get that boy's head checked at Sevier," called James.

One of the boys punched the ignition and the engine roared to life. He put the Cadillac in gear and leaned out the window.

"You Spartanburg boys better not let us catch you over in Greenville County."

"Oh, save it for the Germans." And the deputy threw the straw boater into the backseat where it landed on the unconscious Mark.

As the boys drove away, the owner of the roadhouse shouted from the door, "Hey, they just brought in some new birds."

The deputy, Cleve, and James Stuart all looked at each other.

"Now," asked the deputy, "why couldn't they've brought out those cocks ten minutes ago?"

Cleve and James muttered in agreement.

Returning to the roadhouse, the deputy said, "Stuart, there's something I been meaning to ask you."

"Yeah," said Cleve, chuckling. "Have you ever fired that Webley of yours or is it just an ornament?"

"I've never killed anyone, if that's what you're asking. I have to do business with these people."

The deputy glanced at Cleve. "What I want to know is whether you were on the road a couple of years ago when the McKelvey family ran off that bridge? You always come through selling your guns about that time, but that fall we didn't see you."

Hearing the question, Cleve hung back at the roadhouse door.

"Why would you care?" asked James, looking from one man to the other. "Both of you are Laughlins and it was McKelveys that ended up in the river."

Twenty-four

Katie rode hard and she rode fast, but had the feeling she wouldn't be able to escape the horsemen this time. She shouldn't have returned to the Dark Corner, but return she always did, hanging back in the forest and watching as another family—no relation to her—worked the farm where her family was buried. She'd been fool enough to leave flowers on their graves commemorating the second anniversary of their deaths.

This year they had been waiting for her, and now, as she pushed the mustang through the shadows, the horsemen bore down on her. Another Indian summer, more leaves of red, yellow, and gold, and the sound of hooves behind her. Up ahead was the bridge where she'd lost it all before.

Would she lose everything again, including Mark?

Six months ago, Mark had left to fight the Germans. One month later his letters stopped. The letters stopped to his family, too. Was this why she was out here? Was she intent on joining her dead family because she didn't think Mark would return from the war? Was she intent on joining Mark? Or did she fear that she, too, would become a member of the Old Maids' Club?

Being a tall girl, Katie enjoyed having a man tower over her. Mark had sharp features, was rail-thin, and had wide shoulders. Arms that could easily wrap around her and take her in.

Katie had shivered as they waited for the train. A cold spell had passed through creating a cloudless night and a full moon, and Katie did not miss the opportunity to snuggle into those long arms.

Margaret Belle stood next to her. Aunt Margaret was not pleased. Not only was her niece hugging and kissing in public, but Katie was sending her young man off to war. For this reason, sisters Helen and Mary Kate flatly refused to come down to the station and see the soldiers off.

Mark's parents were there, sharing their oldest child with a girl a bit too bold for their taste. Though Katie was an excellent student who attended Greenville Woman's College and always treated adults with the proper respect, they sensed a wild streak running through her. Katie had been one of the first to bob her hair and wear sleeveless sundresses, requiring underarm shaving. Still, on the plus side, she sewed all her own clothing, and Mark's mother had to admit the girl's jumper of deep blue chiffon embroidered with Chinese medallions around the waist and sleeves had lovely lines. Matching purse, heels, and a broad-brimmed hat turned up at one side completed Katie's stylish look.

For the longest Mark's mother couldn't put her finger on what exactly it was she didn't like about Katie Belle, not until the evening her husband read out loud to the family about the American Indian. Then she knew. There was no real love on Katie's part, only the chance to collect another scalp.

Katie looked up from under her hat. "Take care while you're gone, Mark, and come back to me."

The young man smiled that crooked little smile of his. "I always listen to what you say, Katie dear, ever since you whipped my butt in eighth grade."

Katie smiled up at him. "Oh, how time has affected your memory, sir. You tripped that day or I wouldn't have been able to seize my advantage."

Mark held her out where he could examine Katie's advantage. Where did she get all these smashing outfits? His mother said the patterns came out of *The Delineator*; still, there had been a sense of awe in his mother's explanation

The whistle blew, and Mark turned to his family. He shook hands with his father, hugged his mother and his two siblings, and took Katie into his arms again and kissed her so passionately she thought she might faint. Mark's siblings giggled, and as he joined other stragglers leaping aboard the train, Katie felt the station move around her, the moon shake in the night sky.

Fortunately, Aunt Margaret was there and took her arm. "Wave, my dear. Wave!"

Somehow, Katie found the strength to wave, and smile. Oh, my, but did she smile! The tingle from Mark's kiss reached all the way down to her toes.

The train lurched, and Mark waved from among the

uniforms crowded onto the platform between cars. The scene caused Katie to flash back to the night when she had stood between cars and waved to James Stuart. She was certainly past all that. Nowadays, she had her pick of much more sophisticated young men.

Letters came almost daily while Mark was stateside. He wrote long epistles saying this was a job he had to do. The Germans were sinking ships without warning, murdering Americans onboard. Besides, the war would end once the American Expeditionary Force tipped the balance in favor of the Allies.

Katie wrote daily. She never missed a day. And never missed a day missing Mark. Since mail was delivered twice daily, Katie spent a great deal of time on the porch in one of the rockers. This amused the mailman. He had several lovesick girls along his route.

A few days later a note arrived that had been posted on the day his battalion sailed for Europe. It was filled with his undying devotion for her and his promise to write again when a letter could be sent home.

Oh, Mark, write anytime, write anywhere, and write about anything!

Images of Mark holding her . . . that kiss . . .

The next letter arrived two weeks later, and everyone in Belles Lodging gathered around as Katie stood at the preparation table. Hand at her mouth in fear of what she might read, Katie was informed that Mark's unit had sailed on a confiscated luxury line with six thousand men aboard. The letter went on to explain that the weather had been crystal clear all the way across the Atlantic.

Perfect submarine weather, joked Mark.

No joke for those waiting at home!

Katie dropped the letter and collapsed into the arms of her aunts. At Mark's home in Boyce Lawn, his mother took to bed after reading a copy of the same letter.

The letter went on to add that after a long day at the railing, searching for submarines, Mark and his friends went below and finished the night playing poker. The following day there was more zigging and zagging, endless lifeboat drills and calisthenics, and those bulky life preservers that must be worn at all times. At night the ship was blacked out, all smoking done below deck. It was in this letter that Mark admitted to having taken up smoking to pass the time of day.

"Not good. Not good at all," said Helen, shaking her head.

Katie had taken a seat on one of the stools while Margaret finished reading the letter. Her head snapped up and she stared at her aunt. Helen had suffered through a previous war and smoked! Did Aunt Helen know something she wasn't telling?

Mary Kate put a hand on her shoulder. "All Aunt Helen means is that smoking is a difficult habit to break."

"Yes, yes," agreed Helen, nodding quickly. "You've seen how hard it is for me to stop."

Actually, Katie had never seen her Aunt Helen try to give up tobacco, but that was neither here nor there.

Margaret returned to the letter and Mark's complaints that he could never be a sailor. The ocean was wide and endless, and boring.

Oh, Mark!

He closed with a couple of lines professing his love for her.

That was it? That was all?

Katie thought she'd go out of her mind. This letter was nothing more than a report from a doughboy serving overseas. If she wanted to read real love letters, she'd have to open her hope chest upstairs and unbind his earlier ones.

But that wouldn't be fair to Mark's mother, and as she always did whenever she received a letter, Katie walked over to Boyce Lawn to share her news.

After being informed that Mark's mother had taken to her bed over his comments about German submarines, Katie stalked through downtown, barely seeing two huge signs towering over Main Street. At the corner of Broad stood the Southeastern Life Insurance Company's huge gladiator, and at the corner of Washington a sign read, "Our Country First, then Greenville."

With the opening of Camp Sevier, Main was congested with cars, trucks, trolleys, and the occasional wagon drawn by horses or even cows. All this required policemen directing traffic at the more dangerous intersections.

Katie wove her way through the crowded sidewalks under a tangle of telephone, electric, and trolley car lines. Before the war, where merchants might linger at their doorway to catch a customer's eye, soldiers now vied for Katie's attention. In their smart-looking khaki uniforms, they walked beside her and tried to strike up a conversation.

"How you doing, lady?"

"Need a friend?"

"Need a boyfriend?"

Victoria Lee emerged from the Swandale Building, pulling on her gloves. The Swandale Building, formerly Mansion House Hotel, had been the first hotel constructed in Greenville, a three-story L-shaped structure around two sides of the courthouse square. Carpenter Brothers Drugs occupied a storefront office on the lower level, and Mansion House had recently reopened in support of the soldiers serving at Camp Sevier. When George Roper moved to Greenville, he opened offices in the Swandale; two years later he convinced Victoria Lee to come to work for him, ostensibly to support the war effort.

Victoria saw Katie stalking past the glass doors, followed by more than one soldier trying to catch her eye. Victoria pushed her way through the doors and to the sidewalk.

"Katie! Katie Belle!"

Katie stopped, looked around, and realized where she was.

"Where are you going, my dear?" Victoria wore a tailored suit with a four-gore skirt, back and front seams open below the hip, the coat in loose panels. The long, tight sleeves were fastened with buttons and buttonholes; the shoes barely had heels. Her straw boater's hatband matched the navy blue broadcloth of her suit.

Katie swung around, her hand holding the letter almost hitting one of the soldiers in the face. "It's from Mark." In contrast, Katie wore a pleated skirt of light blue jersey, instep length. At a time when jersey was usually associated with underwear, wherever Katie went people stared, women asking why the Belles couldn't control their niece.

"I hope there's good news."

"It's boring."

A soldier grinned. "We're here, if you're lonely."

"I was thinking of going riding."

"You can ride with us, babe. Bob here has a car."

Victoria took the letter. "Well, no news is good news."

There was talk of romance between Victoria Lee and George Roper, but the only time anyone had ever seen them together was at the Belles for Sunday dinner or sitting on the front porch. George continued to live at the Ottaray, just a few blocks away, and occasionally Katie had been given a ride, but never once had Victoria been seen in the Stutz Bearcat. For this reason, what followed totally astonished Katie.

The trolley rang its bell and stopped. Victoria only exited the Swandale Building when she could see the trolley coming. Good that she did because from behind the trolley came the call of "whore"! Katie tried to turn around, but Victoria eased her, actually pushed the younger woman, onto the trolley.

"You slut!" shouted a male voice.

Onboard the trolley, the women each paid her nickel and sat together so Victoria could read Katie's letter. None of the soldiers was allowed to board. The conductor barred their way.

"Catch the next one, boys. We're full up."

Katie kept her head down, but still the rain of "whore, slut," and now "minx" followed the trolley car down the street, actually followed them to the next stop. There,

Katie dared to look out the rear and saw a young man with an umbrella chasing them. Katie knew there were words, phrases, even situations a lady should ignore, but this young man continued to chase after their trolley, wave his umbrella, and shout: "whore, slut, minx"! Again, the trolley car pulled away before he caught up with them.

How could this be happening on the streets of Greenville? And why would Victoria be the object of such scorn?

"What just happened?" she asked, whispering to the older woman.

"Nothing, my dear," said Victoria, patting the girl's knee. "Just make sure you never divorce your husband. Some people don't take it very well."

Three weeks later another letter arrived, this one informing Katie of the reception received by the American Expeditionary Force upon arriving in Brest, France. Bands played, ships and boats blew their whistles, and crowds lined the shore. Everywhere Mark looked, people were waving American flags.

But to the north of them, less than four hundred miles away, the most vicious fighting of the war was taking place. After the communists pulled Russia out of the conflict, Germany had been able to turn its energies against the Allies, and the British commander issued his famous order: "With our backs to the wall, and believing in the justice of our cause, each one of us must fight on to the end!"

Still, the German offensive did not materialize, and looking back on the combat readiness of both sides, it may have been an attack of influenza that halted the German advance.

No one back home knew about the flu as papers on both sides of the conflict reported only the good news. But Spain was neutral, and her newspapers weren't under such restrictions. Here the flu received its name and raced across Europe, then set sail for America, jumping from one camp to another. Greenville would not be immune.

While the fighting went on to the north of them and soldiers on both sides were crippled by the flu, Mark and his fellow soldiers enjoyed French bread, French wine, and especially French women. When Mark eventually wrote again, he informed Katie that French cognac was absolutely tops and that the Yankee dollar went much farther there than back in the States.

Mark never penned a line about the women, but they were there, approaching the doughboys right up to the moment when the Americans reached the front lines. Seven weeks later, the letters stopped, and all Katie could think of was how she'd allowed Mark to go off to war.

Why hadn't she made him marry her? She could be pregnant with his child! Now all she had was a few crummy letters and the memory of Mark waving from between passenger cars, just as she'd waved to James Stuart two years earlier.

The wagon approaching on the far side of the bridge had a canvas top similar to the one Katie had hidden under two years ago, and here it was, magically reappearing under the red, gold, and yellow roof of the autumn forest. No matter whose wagon it was, Katie decided to beat the wagon crossing the bridge, putting a barrier between her and her three pursuers.

Katie raced full bore for the turn, leaning to one side of Devil and whispering encouragement. Then there were hoof beats on the wooden planking, and instead of faltering like her family's horse had when pulling their carriage, the mustang righted itself and charged for the far side of the bridge.

Katie leaned forward, slapping the reins. It would be close, but the wagoneer must have seen them coming because he was pulling back on his reins. His face looked familiar—it was James!—and as soon as they passed, Katie heard him slap his reins, forcing his wagon across the bridge and into the path of the oncoming horsemen.

Katie glanced over her shoulder and saw the horsemen pull to a stop, their horses fighting to avoid the wagon. On her side of the bridge, she gripped her reins and the mustang reared up, snorting and pawing the air. Once she had Devil under control, Katie returned to the bridge and watched the argument developing between James and her pursuers. From where she sat astride the mustang, Katie could not see the river and she actually never gave it another thought.

There were only two horsemen now, one of them, the one wearing the cowboy hat, shouting and gesticulating at the wagoneer to move his rig, the other guiding his mount to where he could peer over the side of the bridge. When the two horsemen separated, Katie saw the third horse behind them, now riderless.

James ignored the shouts and the gesticulations of the rider in the cowboy hat, threw on the brake, and climbed down from the driver's box. From the rear of the wagon, he took a coil of rope.

A horn startled Katie and she guided her horse from the path of the roadway, allowing a truck to pull through and halt at the edge of the bridge. Leaving the engine running, the driver pulled on his brake, got out, and started across on foot.

Earl Laughlin stepped back from the edge and shook his head. "Andrew, you damn fool." To James, he said, "Rebecca and I are leaving for the mill village day after tomorrow."

James stepped to the edge of the ravine and saw Andrew Laughlin lying facedown in the shallows. "I just wish you'd made that decision a few hours ago." He handed one end of the rope to Earl.

Earl took the rope and tied it around him. "Wouldn't have made much difference. Andrew's thrown in with Cleve." He nodded in the direction of the man wearing the cowboy hat. His cousin was tying up the horses. "Besides, the factory couldn't send the wagon until next week." He fitted a bowline under his shoulders and glanced across the bridge. "I'm getting out before the Bloomer Babe gets me. That girl carries a grudge."

By now, James had his end of the rope looped around the horn of Earl's saddle and he encouraged the horse to dig in with its hooves. Earl started down backwards, with James playing out the rope and keeping up a gentle stream of patter with the horse.

The driver of the truck reached their side of the bridge and looked over the railing. "What happened?"

"Riding too fast to make the turn."

"You were blocking the way," said the man wearing the cowboy hat. Cleve Laughlin joined them at the edge of the ravine and watched his cousin work his way down the side.

"I was already on the bridge," said James, playing out the rope. "Why didn't you slow down when you saw me coming?"

"You pulled on the bridge to block us."

"What?" asked the truck driver, looking from the man with the snake on his hat to the one playing out the rope.

"Steady, boy, steady." Of Cleve, James asked, "I blocked you?"

The rope went limp, meaning Earl had reached the bottom of the ravine.

"Now why would I do that?"

"'Cause you're in cahoots with the Bloomer Babe."

"A baby?" The truck driver glanced at the man lying in the shallows. The man did not move when his brother knelt beside him and shook his shoulder. "There's a baby down there?"

"No, no! The Bloomer Babe!" Cleve pointed at the figure in white across the bridge.

On the other side of the ravine, Katie pulled back on her reins, causing the mustang to rear up on its hind legs. Cleve cursed her and returned to his horse.

"Cocky wench," commented the truck driver.

"Idiot," commented James.

The rope went tight, and he started backing the horse away from the ravine, hauling up the two men.

"What kind of horse is that?" asked the truck driver,

staring at the figure across the bridge.

"Mustang," said James, much too quickly. He glanced at Cleve, returning with a rifle. "At least it looks like a mustang from here." James increased the pull of the horse.

"A mustang this side of the Mississippi?" asked the driver as James and Earl's horse backed farther and farther away.

The truck driver gave Earl a hand when the two men came up, and they laid out the injured man while James released the rope, left Earl's horse, and headed for the wagon.

On the bridge, between the railing and James's wagon, Cleve took up a position with his rifle. Across the bridge, Katie saw the weapon, went low in the saddle, and guided Devil away. In white, she was a conspicuous target against a background of autumn colors.

James put a shoulder into Cleve, and Cleve stumbled forward, his weapon discharging harmlessly into the bridge. James's horse neighed and tried to back away.

"Sorry about that. Tripped."

Laughlin snorted, stepped forward, and raised the rifle again.

"Hey, that's my truck over there." The driver came up behind Cleve as he snapped off a shot in the direction of the rider.

James had the harness of the wagon now, speaking gently to the horse, soothing the animal with his words and his hand.

The truck driver grabbed the rifle and pushed it down. "What the hell's wrong with you? I said, that's my truck."

Cleve pulled back on the rifle, recovering control of it. When he looked again, the rider was gone. "She rides through here like she owns the damn place."

"Maybe she does. You haven't been able to catch her." James prepared to climb into the driver's box.

Laughlin put a hand on his shoulder. "I'm not finished with you yet, Stuart."

James faced him, hand on the butt of the Webley. "I said I hadn't killed anyone, Cleve, but in your case, I'm willing to make an exception."

"What's wrong with you people?" asked the truck driver. "A man needs to be pulled from the river and you two are busy jabbering about some girl. It don't make no sense."

"Well," said James, nose to nose with Cleve Laughlin, "you are in the darkest corner of the state."

The truck driver stomped back across the bridge. "Move that wagon, would you? I'd like to make my stops and get the hell out of here."

Cleve watched James settle into the driver's box. "I don't know why people don't just order from Montgomery Ward."

"Probably because revenuers can track the amount of sugar you order through Ward's."

Cleve snorted and returned to where his cousin knelt beside his brother. When the wagon passed the three Laughlins, James was not asked to place Andrew in the wagon or carry him anywhere. Neither was the truck driver, which could only mean Andrew Laughlin was dead.

TWENTY-FIVE

The pilots flying out of Camp Sevier were your usual jaunty lot, but only Herbert Mitchum took Katie seriously when she said she'd like to learn to fly. Mitchum told Katie she must come up with the money, not only for the lessons, but for the fuel and he would indeed teach her how to fly.

They stood beside a de Havilland DH.4, a wooden biplane with two widely spaced cockpits separated by the fuel tank. Communication between the two cockpits, as Katie was about to learn, was next to nil, even through the plane did have a speaking tube. Mitchum's hand gripped one strut as he leaned down toward her and Katie's hands held her small hat as if it were still the large, wide-brimmed, pre-war fashion she used to hold to create a barrier between herself and the young men gathering around her.

And Katie was something to stare at. She wore a long-sleeved blouse and a pair of trousers she'd sewn, patterned after a pair of Robert Patton's pants with suspenders. Her shoes were sensibly laced, with round toes and low-wedge heels.

"Oh, I have the money. I learned shorthand and typing at the Woman's College. I'm a stenographer for Southern Bell and a reporter for the *Piedmont.*"

Mitchum was amused. "So when do you have time to go dancing, Miss Belle?"

"I dance Saturday nights with the soldiers at the YMCA."

"You make it sound like a chore." He bent down still holding onto the strut. "I hope you set aside a little time for romance."

Katie stepped back. "I'm betrothed."

The flyer straightened up. "My apologies, Miss Belle. I saw no ring."

"My boyfriend's overseas." From the neck of her blouse, Katie fished Mark's class ring on her mother's silver chain, then returned it inside her blouse. "I want to earn my license before they close down the army base."

"Oh, I'm sure you've plenty of time. The war's just beginning."

Mitchum knew aviatrixes were not uncommon. Harriet Quimby, America's first female pilot, had crossed the English Channel; Katherine Stinson had given up a career as a concert pianist; and crazy Ruth Law not only flew but walked on wings! But a Southern girl? You take one of these belles up and you'd better squeeze in another passenger to grab her when she wants to jump out of the plane.

Mitchum had toyed with signing up for overseas duty, perhaps even with the Canadians, but stateside duty offered many more girls who'd thrill at his barrel rolls, loop-the-loops, and upside-down flying; young women willing to meet you later that night and explore other forms of excitement besides dancing. When America declared war on Germany, Mitchum was hired to fly mail routes. But stationed at Sevier, which Mitchum considered a real backwater—South Carolina didn't have a legitimate airstrip in the whole damned state—once again he toyed with the idea of volunteering for overseas duty; that is, until another Katie Belle came along. And they always came along. Belle was just another of those round-heeled girls who thought they could do anything men could do, including having sex.

The first step in Mitchum's seduction process was to take the girl up and see what she was all about. The worst that could come of that would be the two of them chumming it up on the ground after Belle became seduced by the thrill of flying.

But Katie was serious and coughed up four hundred dollars for twenty lessons. She also demanded a receipt outlining his responsibilities to her. And when he was invited for Sunday dinner, Mitchum recognized a kindred spirit. Katie was an orphan being raised by three old maid aunts while Mitchum had been raised by an aunt and uncle who sent him out on the street to sell newspapers, shovel coal, and clean up after horses.

When he wasn't given any of the money, he ran off with the circus, and somewhere along the way, learned how to fly. That led to one affair after another and a rather careless attitude toward women. Not that Mitchum expected Katie to skedaddle with him. The ones who formed any attachment, he'd pulled a fade on, which was as easy as turning the prop on his plane.

To his surprise, Katie turned out to be an excellent student. Still, that didn't mean she wouldn't fall for this dashing young aviator if the proper circumstances arose. Betty Jean had gone up with Katie for her first ride and wet her pants. After that, it made more sense to Betty Jean to remain on the ground and flirt with the other pilots. For a girl looking for someone to love, the new military camp just north of Greenville was heaven-sent.

While Betty Jean studied the pilots, Katie Belle learned, both on the ground and in the air, that the rudder bar and the stick were connected to the controls in the aft cockpit. Every movement made by the student was duplicated in the instructor's cockpit. Mitchum remained in charge of the plane at all times.

Mitchum went on to explain, with drawings and in the air, that piloting an aircraft differed from driving a car in that pilots also need to watch their lateral control. Whereas, cars turn corners and go up and down hills, drivers never really worry about whether the wheels remained on the road. Not so for a plane. A pilot has the additional responsibility of keeping the wings level.

The first time Katie pushed the rudder bar forward, she was elated at the response. Oh, my, but this was exciting! The wind in her face, the roar of the engine, breaking free of the earth's gravity. She was soaring through the air like . . .

The plane was flying sideways!

Planes couldn't fly sideways.

Maybe if she turned the stick or pushed on the bar . . . Oh, God, that's what she should've done: push the bar forward and turn the stick. She'd lost traction.

No, no! Planes don't grip the air—which is why they go faster than cars. But airplanes can lift. That's how they become airborne!

But moving sideways like they were, the aircraft blocks the flow of air over the wings!

Correction! Blocks the air over one wing! That's why the plane was falling. She needed to put some air under her wings and lift the plane. But when she gripped the stick there was no response. The stick wouldn't move. It was stuck!

She wanted to ask Mitchum for advice, like she'd asked one of her aunts while being taught how to drive, but strapped in the cockpit, she couldn't get her head or the leather helmet and goggles around. Releasing the stick, the stick suddenly moved, as did the rudder bar.

Oh, God! That's Mitchum. He's flying the plane!

Katie sagged into her seat, and as she watched, the plane rolled in the direction of the turn as the rudder yawed the plane around and a stream of air was forced over the wings, exchanging drag for lift.

Once they had leveled out, Mitchum explained what he had done, adding in short shouts, "That's what the hours are for. You've got to learn to deal with every situation so you don't have to think when an emergency arises."

Katie understood what she'd done, and before long, asked to take control of the aircraft once again.

For the remainder of the lesson, Katie concentrated on using the stick to tip the wings up or down, and, of course, the real fun, pulling back on the stick and soaring off into the wild blue yonder. That is, if you didn't gain altitude so fast the engine conked out.

Suddenly, they were falling . . . backwards.

Falling to earth!

The engine had stopped, and all she could hear was the rush of wind whistling past her.

Now it was Katie's turn to wet *her* pants.

"Got it! Got it!" shouted Mitchum from behind her.

The engine fired up, the propeller began to turn, and moments later, Mitchum righted the plane.

He laughed from behind her. "Remind me never to turn over the aircraft to you, Miss Belle, unless we're at least at a thousand feet."

Katie couldn't speak. To be in a plane when the engine stopped frightened her more than racing through the Dark Corner pursued by her family's murderers.

As the twenty-lesson plan came to an end, Mitchum grounded them in the middle of nowhere with engine trouble.

Well, Mitchum thought they were in the middle of nowhere, but Katie had no intention of spending the night in a cotton field with Herbert Mitchum.

She took a reading by the stars, just as her father had taught her, and after a couple of hours they reached Blind Switch, the former plantation home of the Belle family. There they borrowed a horse, and Katie and Herbert rode up Old Stage Road, passing more than one motor car stalled out beside the road. That, however, wasn't how Mitchum played it.

The following morning when Katie arrived at Camp Sevier to make arrangements to return the borrowed horse, she learned Mitchum was riding the horse to

Blind Switch so he could retrieve his plane.

"Sorry, Miss Belle," said one of the pilots. "Didn't Mitchum explain he works for the post office, flying mail from one city to another? He was overdue to leave and packed a bag this morning and left on horseback."

"But last night when we lost . . ."

The pilots smirked at each other. They knew what had been lost last night. Herbert Mitchum had kept them up, regaling them with his latest conquest.

Katie realized with horror what the talk would be. "Are you telling me . . .?"

She turned away as tears appeared in her eyes. In her head, she heard James Stuart: Actions have consequences.

Katie exhaled. Well, if there were to be consequences, she would be the one to create them.

One of the pilots put a hand on her shoulder. If Mitchum had broken in this girl last night, perhaps she'd be amenable to another evening flight.

Katie threw off his hand and stalked out of the building. The two pilots were still laughing over what a delightful cad Herbert Mitchum was when one of their mechanics strolled into the office wiping his hands with a greasy rag.

"Sir, it's not my place to question your judgment, but do you really think the Belle girl's ready to solo? She's only got twenty hours under her belt."

The pilots bolted upright in their chairs. "What in the world are you talking about?" asked one of them.

"Belle asked me to turn her prop. I thought you'd at least want to watch her take off. You really are cool characters. I'd be chewing on my tongue."

The pilots raced outside. Like the mechanic said, Katie was soloing, and as the "borrowed" plane bumped along, heading for the runway, the pilots chased after her.

To no avail. Once the plane reached the runway, Katie turned into the wind, opened the throttle, and moments later, was airborne.

The mechanic leaped into the Buick and chased after the pilots. When they returned to the flight office, the phone was ringing off the hook.

"Who authorized that flight?" yelled a voice over the line. "I've told you pilots this office is to receive the proper paperwork whenever you take out a plane. You think fuel grows on trees?"

The pilots looked at each other, one holding the receiver so the other could hear.

"Well?" demanded the officer on the other end of the line. "I bounced Mitchum for doing this, and I'm here to tell you if there's one thing we don't need at Sevier it's more joyriders."

"I'll have the paperwork sent right over, sir," said one of the pilots. "I don't know why it wasn't filed with your office."

"Very well. Now in case the general asks, where shall I say that plane is headed?"

The pilots looked at each other. One of them gritted his teeth and said, "Blind Switch."

"Blind Switch? Where the hell's Blind Switch?"

Katie arrived at the pasture where their plane had experienced "engine trouble" the night before. Along the way, she buzzed a man on horseback. Once she observed Mitchum returning the horse to Blind Switch, she put her plane down nose-to-nose with Mitchum's and waited.

The pilot was smiling as he climbed over the last fence and strolled out to the planes. "Surprised to see you, Katie."

"I didn't pay four hundred dollars for nothing."

"I taught you how to fly."

Katie produced a sheet of paper from her purse. "You failed to sign the paperwork for my license."

"Well, my dear, you had not soloed by then."

"I have now."

Katie pulled off the leather helmet and shook out her hair while Mitchum looked over the paperwork.

"It says here you must have more than one licensed pilot sign off on this. I don't think you'll find another pilot willing to sign off." Mitchum grinned at her. "Not unless you're willing to pay for more lessons."

Katie gestured at a plane circling overhead. The two pilots from Camp Sevier had followed her to Laurens County.

"Oh, I think I have more than enough pilots who wish to put a second signature to that paperwork. Girls who can fly acquire their own set of camp followers."

Twenty-six

"Mama, will Mr. Roper make a good father?" Betty Jean sat with her mother on the bed.

"You have only one father, Betty Jean. Edmund Lee."

"But now I'm to have two."

"George Roper will be your stepfather."

"You love him more than you love Father. You'll love him more than you love me."

"Nonsense. I love George . . . differently."

Betty Jean took her mother's hand, the one with the engagement ring. "This is an expensive diamond. You'll have to love him more."

"Betty Jean, I don't know where you get some of your ideas."

Her daughter dropped the hand. "I was surprised that Mr. Roper picked you, that's all."

"Betty Jean, don't be silly."

"I'm not being silly. You're so serious. Work and church, work and church. That's all you do."

"Being a lady is a serious business, my dear."

"Actually, it appears rather tiresome."

Victoria rolled her eyes.

"Mother, you must become more fun-loving. George will expect that. George has a sense of humor."

"Mr. Roper to you, my dear."

Betty Jean got up from the bed and swept gracefully across the room. "This is you, so elegant."

She turned around, swishing back across the room, this time moving her bottom. "This is me, and I know which one boys like."

"Betty Jean! That is cheap and coarse. Never walk in such a manner again. I forbid it."

Her daughter returned to her seat. "You're so prissy. I have no idea why anyone would call you a whore."

Victoria's mouth dropped open and she slapped her daughter's face. Realizing what she'd done, Victoria burst into tears, put her arms around her daughter, and pulled her close.

"Oh, darling, I'm so sorry. I didn't mean—"

"Of course you did." Betty Jean broke out of her mother's embrace. "I know things you don't want me to know. Bad girls have more fun, and that's why you won George Roper, not some virgin." Her daughter left the room, slamming the door behind her.

Down the hallway, Betty Jean rapped on the toilet door, and finding no one there, went inside, sat on the commode, and began to cry. First, she'd lost her father, now her mother. Where would she find someone who'd love her?

✣ ✣ ✣

The Sunday following the incident of the man with the umbrella chasing the trolley, Victoria and George remained at the table after dessert, talking. Occasionally, George would take her hand and squeeze it.

"George, why is this man so angry with me? I don't know what I did to upset him."

"He sees himself as an anchor of morality in a changing world."

"But why? Who appointed him?"

"Everyone did, my dear, even you."

Victoria pulled away. "What . . . what did I do?"

"You didn't speak up against temperance or what followed."

"Please don't tell me you're against temperance." Victoria was a member of the Women's Christian Temperance Union, second only in her passion to the suffrage movement.

"I'm from Charleston, Victoria. If you want to take a drink, you do. That's even true of Columbia and Florence, but things are quite a bit different in the upstate."

Before Victoria agreed to an engagement, several issues had to be resolved. Victoria was a "dry," George a "wet"; Victoria a Republican, George a Democrat; she a Unionist, but as far as George could see, Washington was shoving programs down the throats of Americans with their graduated income tax, a Federal Reserve to control the money supply, and passing a law prohibiting child labor. What company could survive all that?

As to the matter of "wet" versus "dry," the couple decided their house would be dry except in George's study where the liquor cabinet would reside. Since

Victoria had no interest in George's study, just as he had none in her kitchen, the wet and dry issues were nonstarters. And since women could not vote, his fiancée's choosing to be Republican, Democrat, or even a Socialist gave her husband not a moment's worth of concern.

But someone going around town calling his intended a whore, that *was* a concern, and despite his cleverness, George did not know how to handle the problem. You didn't challenge a man carrying an umbrella to a duel; it sounded too quixotic, and the mill took up much of George's time.

Victoria went to the Swandale Building each day and attended church whenever the doors were open. Still, the young man with the umbrella sought her out wherever she went. He was getting on people's nerves. The rector of Christ Church even complained to the chief of police.

But because the young man kept his distance from George and the authorities, and Victoria forbade George's former mother-in-law from informing George of the occasions when the young man did appear, the name-calling continued. Fannie Archibald, recently moved to the upcountry with her two grandchildren and living in an adjoining suite at the Ottaray, wondered what effect the name-calling was having on their fellow Greenvillians?

Who was this man?

It was rumored he had beaten a colored man to death in Possum Kingdom. Another rumor held that he had owned a failed umbrella business in Columbia. And there was the rumor that he was the son of someone

George Roper had killed in the Dark Corner. Since George spent little time in that part of the county, the last rumor was given little credence.

Yet no one was prepared for what happened when George came to town to take his fiancée to lunch. Victoria, who was usually so careful whenever she left the Swandale Building, was immediately set upon by the man with the umbrella. Mrs. Archibald had called her former son-in-law back to the office on a business matter.

Realizing her husband-to-be would be coming out the door right behind her, Victoria retreated to the lobby. This only emboldened her harasser and he followed her inside. When George caught up with Victoria in the lobby, heard the name-calling, and saw the umbrella waved at his fiancée, he snatched the umbrella from the young man's hand and threw it across the lobby.

Startled, the young man backed off. But once George and Victoria left the building, he picked up the umbrella and followed them into the street, where he resumed his verbal assault in front of a lunchtime crowd.

When the young man called Victoria a whore, George pulled his pistol. "Call that back or you'll be the next on the ground."

Instead, the name-caller waved his umbrella and proclaimed that George and his fiancée were on a fast train to hell.

George put one bullet in the man's chest, and the man crumpled to his knees, fell forward, and expired on the spot.

Victoria rushed to his side.

Angered that this scarlet woman would dare touch

him, his last words were: "You . . . you . . . go . . . to . . ."

George was taken into custody, Victoria went into seclusion at Belles Lodging, and Roper and Sons in Charleston became aware that a textile mill in the upcountry bore their name.

At the trial George was represented by lawyers from two law firms, one a colonel who fought on the side of the North, the other a major who had fought for the South. Ordinarily, the colonel would outrank the major, but this being the South, the colonel deferred to the major, who had ridden with Wade Hampton.

The jury was all male and all white. Katie Belle, reporting for the *Piedmont,* sat in the gallery with the other reporters, but the three old maids forbade her to interview Victoria while under their roof. Sanctuary meant sanctuary, especially at Belles Lodging.

The editor of the *Piedmont* did not know this when he had hired the girl. Katie took shorthand faster than his most experienced secretary, and she could fly a plane! A girl like this didn't come along every day, not to mention she had the inside track with the fiancée of the accused.

Katie's new job caused a schism to develop between Betty Jean and her. Betty Jean refused to speak to her former friend. Besides, it wasn't fair for Katie to have a job that put her in contact with so many attractive young men. Why didn't good things ever happen to her?

The police learned the victim belonged to every

church in town, and had been asked to leave every church in town, including several Negro churches. When his apartment was searched, it was found to contain boxes and boxes of umbrellas but no weapons. The Umbrella Man, as Katie referred to him in her reports for the *Piedmont,* opposed the Jim Crow laws, was a strong Union man, and a prohibitionist. Every Monday he had stood outside the courthouse and waved his umbrella, proclaiming his intention to rid Greenville of card players, wets, and tango dancers.

The prosecution produced witnesses from both the staff of the Swandale Building and the passersby on Main Street who had witnessed the shooting. The colonel and the major cross-examined all these witnesses and only a few were discredited. Instead, the defense made the point that the man with the umbrella had besmirched the reputation of a respected woman of this fair city and repeatedly threatened her with a weapon. In shooting this man, though only armed with an umbrella, George Roper was defending his fiancée's honor, and the defense paraded a line of character witnesses before the jury.

And each night, when the judge went home, his wife warned him that no one would marry Mrs. Lee if her fiancé was convicted of murder. Since her family in Ohio would have little to do with her, Mrs. Lee would always remain a loose woman wandering the streets of Greenville.

The following day, the judge requested Victoria to join him in chambers.

"Mrs. Lee, this court is willing to show you every

courtesy by allowing you and James Stuart to leave by a side door, but there is still the question . . ."

"Yes, your honor?"

"You are standing by your man at this moment, but do you plan to remain in Greenville at the conclusion of the trial?"

Victoria's face tightened. "Your honor, I have been abandoned by my husband and disowned by my family. My daughter and I live as we do because of the kindness of strangers. For this reason, Betty Jean and I call no other place home."

When George Roper returned for the afternoon session, the judge ordered all the principals into his chamber, along with James Stuart. Once the door closed, the clerk offered George the chance to take the oath.

"Your honor," objected the former major of the Confederacy, "this is highly irregular."

"Henry, it's an open-and-shut case of murder. How much can I possibly hurt your client's cause?"

"Your honor, there are—"

"I'll take the oath," said George, raising his hand and facing the clerk.

"George, I do not recommend—"

"Oh, please shut up, Henry," said the judge, "before I forget you fought on our side during the war."

The courthouse was packed and the streets overrun with those waiting for some word on the trial. Negroes treated the affair like a visit from the circus and were making money hand over fist, but fights still broke out and the new jail kept filling with those who, in a county that had voted itself dry, had become drunk and disorderly overnight.

"Any objections?" the judge asked of the prosecutor.

The prosecutor, a young man who had not fought in any wars, said, "Your honor, I have no objection to this ceremony." Born and raised in the state, the prosecutor understood that South Carolina had been created to turn a profit, and no profits could be turned if you didn't have peace and good order. The fights and disorderly conduct must cease.

The oath was administered, and George faced the judge.

"Do you plan to marry Mrs. Lee after the trial?"

"It depends on whether Mrs. Lee will have me."

"So you'd take Mrs. Lee to be your lawfully wedded wife?"

"Absolutely!"

The judge turned to the open door leading to his honor's private washroom. He raised his voice. "Mrs. Lee, will you take this man to be your lawfully wedded husband?"

Victoria came through the door, trailed by Katie Belle. Both women were beaming. "Certainly, your honor. I mean, I do."

The clerk pulled flowers from a vase on the judge's desk and handed them to Victoria. The judge motioned her to stand in front of his desk with Katie Belle at her side.

"Mr. Stuart?"

"Sir?" came the reply from the rear of chambers.

"We need a best man."

"Yes, sir." Stuart hustled forward where he was given a thin clip of metal. "What's this?"

"A paperclip," explained the clerk.

"It clips paper?" asked the gun salesman.

"Just give Mr. Roper the clip. He'll know what to do with it."

George took the paperclip, bent it into a rough circle, and fitted the thin piece of metal around Victoria's ring finger. Katie took the flowers from the bride's hands and smiled across the happy couple to James Stuart.

"Any objections to pronouncing these two husband and wife?" asked the judge.

There were none.

"I now pronounce you husband and wife." Smiling, he added, "You may kiss the bride."

George did, and South Carolina recognized its first divorce, albeit de facto.

"Now, back to business!"

In the courtroom, summations were made and the case went to the jury. A half hour later, the jury returned a verdict of guilty, and the judge sentenced George Roper to time served and a fine that would include more work for James Stuart.

"Mr. Stuart," said the judge from the bench, "since you appear to have an uncommon knowledge of the Dark Corner, I charge you—and you are to do this within thirty days—to locate the mother or the wife of the victim and deliver the first check written by Mr. Roper."

"A check, your honor?" asked Roper, straightening up from where he had leaned over the railing and hugged Victoria.

"Mr. Roper, you are to write a personal check for

fifty dollars every month for the rest of this woman's life, whether she's the mother or the man's wife, and mail it to a post office box opened and maintained at your expense. There, the woman can pick up the check and request an officer from the police or sheriff's department to escort her to the bank, department store, or hardware store of her choice."

"Your honor," argued the former Confederate major, "be reasonable."

"Henry, you can always appeal." To George, the judge said, "The man you shot down may have been crazy as a bedbug, but someone, somewhere, is depending on his income, now and in the future."

The judge's settlement caused women, young and old, to beg for support from George Roper, one plea coming from as far away as east Texas. The discovery of the Saluda River mill owned by Roper and Sons of Charleston was another skeleton to fall out of George Roper's closet. The publicity from the trial did that.

Twenty-seven

One day when Victoria had her head in the mill's accounting, three men presented themselves at the Greenville office of Roper and Sons. Dressed in black suits, each had a pasty complexion and held a homburg hat. One of them carried a briefcase and wore glasses; another cleared his throat to get Victoria's attention.

"Oh," she said, scrambling to her feet on the other side of the counter, "pardon me, sir. I didn't see you standing there."

The leader of the three gave Victoria a short nod. "Quite all right, miss." He inclined his head in the direction of an older woman on the far side of a glass door leading to another room. The older woman was talking on the telephone and another phone could be heard ringing. She did not appear to see them.

"Busy office," commented the man.

"Oh, well, it's the war, you know."

"Lots of orders?" he asked.

"I think you'd best ask Mr. Roper about that."

"That's why we're here—to see Mr. Roper."

"Oh." Victoria glanced at her desk. "Did you have an appointment?" She fingered the paperclip on the breast of her blouse, it having been replaced by a gold ring on her finger.

"We don't need an appointment," said the man with the briefcase. "This is Samuel Roper, senior partner of Roper and Sons of Charleston."

"Oh. Well, George isn't here. He's at the mill." She reached for the phone. "Shall I call him for you?"

Samuel Roper reached over the counter and turned the ledger around so he could read the numbers. "You keep the books for George?"

"Oh, yes," said Victoria, "but I'm not authorized to discuss figures. You would have to speak with Mr. Roper about that."

Samuel Roper picked up the heavy journal and laid it on the counter. He ran his finger down one column, then another.

"Sir," said Victoria, sternly, "that information is confidential."

The older woman on the phone stared through the glass at the scene taking place at the counter. She said something into one of the phones, hung up, and left the other phone ringing while she opened the glass door and marched into the room. She bustled her way between the counter and the three men and seized the journal.

"Sir," she said, slamming shut the journal, "you have no right to read my son-in-law's journals."

"Oh, Mrs. Archibald," said Victoria, "they're from

Roper and Sons of Charleston." Victoria fingered the paperclip again.

"You're George's mother-in-law?" asked Samuel Roper. "I heard you'd moved to Greenville. How are your grandchildren?"

"The welfare of my grandchildren is my son-in-law's responsibility, not Roper and Sons. Now, would you please leave?"

"Mrs. Archibald, we've come to examine the books." For some reason, Samuel Roper still smiled.

The man wearing glasses and carrying the briefcase said, "We shall need to see all the paperwork regarding this concern." He gestured to the third man. "Mr. Elliott has a subpoena. Mr. Elliott is a specialist in tax law."

Mr. Elliott produced the subpoena from his coat pocket and handed it to the older woman.

Victoria stepped back, horrified. All of this had happened before when she had been married to Edmund—and four days ago she had married George with their honeymoon set for later in the month. How could she be such a fool?

"Victoria, did you hear me?" asked Mrs. Archibald, clutching the journal to her chest, the subpoena in her free hand. "I said call the police and have these men escorted from this office."

"Now, now," said Samuel, "no reason to have a tiff."

"Victoria, are you going to call the police or not?"

The new Mrs. Roper looked at Mrs. Archibald, then at the three men on the other side of the counter.

No, she would not call the police. The last time the police had been sent for they had arrested her!

Victoria picked up her purse, hurried around the counter, and headed for the door.

"Victoria!" shouted her mother-in-law.

"Sorry to upset her," said Samuel Roper, smiling again, "but we still need to see those records."

Victoria flew down the steps, almost running into James Stuart.

"Oh," said the young man, backing away. "Mr. Roper sent me to see if you would like to bring lunch out to the mill. He has something to show you."

"And I have something to tell him," said Victoria.

She marched out of the Swandale Building and over to where the Stutz Bearcat was parked at the curb. Pushing her way through the people gathered around the yellow car, she climbed in, closed the door, and waited impatiently for Stuart to join her.

James followed her to the car. "Er . . . Mrs. Roper, is Mrs. Archibald accompanying us?"

"Mrs. Archibald is busy at the moment, and I have pressing business with my husband, so, if you don't mind . . ."

"Er . . . right." James joined her in the car, pushed the ignition button, and once the vehicle fired up, backed into the street, careful not to run over someone admiring the car.

Saluda Mill was made up of several buildings: a factory two stories tall, each floor with a fifteen-foot ceiling, a picker building, a dye house, boiler room, and engine house. The factory had over eleven thousand spindles and three-hundred sixty looms producing muslin, chambray, camlet, and denim. Rows of houses had been built for the workers, who numbered almost four hundred.

Before James and Victoria arrived at the front gate, Betty Jean was showing one of the company houses to Earl Laughlin, his wife, Rebecca, and their two boys. Rebecca had heard about these houses and now she was about to live in one. Though the house was plain and simple, so was her sharecropper home, and this house had running water, though no tub or commode.

What did that matter? She'd been using an outhouse since childhood. Every outhouse contained a Sears, Roebuck catalogue, and she hated it when important pages disappeared. Sears sold the most beautiful clothing in the whole world.

There was a coal stove where she could cook.

And lights! This girl said the company turned on the electricity every night; all day Wednesday so a woman could get her ironing done.

A bulb hung from the ceiling! No more kerosene lanterns. And with regular deliveries of ice, she could have an icebox and they could have cold drinks instead of having to leave drinks in the spring and wonder if someone would steal them, and, of course, never return the empties.

Rebecca clapped her hands in glee. "How much does this all cost?" It was her husband's question to ask, but it tumbled from her mouth.

"A dollar a week," said Betty Jean. Every day she made couples happy but never pleased herself. Now that her mother had moved in with Mr. Roper, she lived alone at Belles Lodging, and Katie was gone all the time, covering stories for the *Piedmont* or taking dictation at Southern Bell. Why did good things never happen to her?

"Oh, no," argued Rebecca, "a dollar a week can't be true. My sister rents a house in Spartanburg—of course, she doesn't live in a mill village—and her husband pays twenty dollars a month."

"It's true, and you can have your rent, coal, and ice deducted from your husband's paycheck." Deductions meant the husband couldn't drink up his paycheck before reaching home.

Mechanically, Betty Jean added, "And if you work third shift, all you have to do is hang a do-not-disturb sign on your doorknob."

"Third shift?" asked one of the boys.

"Midnight to eight a.m.," replied Betty Jean. "The mill never stops running, except on Sundays." Returning her attention to the adults, she added, "There's a company store where you can purchase clothes, shoes, and groceries. There's a YMCA, a nurse visits once a week, and we have moving pictures Saturday afternoons and Saturday nights."

"Moving pictures?" asked Rebecca.

"Pictures that move," explained Betty Jean.

Rebecca looked at her husband. "I've never seen a moving picture before."

"Not only that. The company's digging a swimming pool."

This broke Earl Laughlin out of his trance. They *had* made the right decision to leave their farm. Seed and fertilizer cost more than you could make, and brewing moonshine brought you nothing but a bunch of nosey revenuers. Or some damned accident.

"You swim in a hole dug in the ground?" asked Earl. "Won't it get dirty with all those people swimming in it?"

"Oh, no," said Betty Jean, laughing, "we'll clean it every week." When Laughlin didn't appear to understand, Betty Jean added, "The interior of the pool will be lined with concrete."

"And church?" asked Rebecca.

"We have a community hall for church, Sunday school, and other events, but land's been set aside for each church. The Presbyterians are already building one."

Lord, thought Rebecca, they *had* died and gone to heaven. No longer would she have to slop hogs, hoe corn, or pick cotton.

There came a knock at the door, it swung open, and four men began to unload a wagon with all their wordly possessions. The wagon had been provided by the company, and it had appeared with these four men at eight o'clock in front of their home. In less than a half hour, all the furniture, boxes, and useless kerosene lamps had been moved into the new house. Tied to the rear of the wagon were the family cow and Earl's horse.

"We have a community pasture for your horse and cow, Mr. Laughlin."

"Sell them!" thundered Earl. "This is home now."

Before the yellow car stopped in front of the mill office, Victoria had the door open.

"Mrs. Lee!" said Stuart, startled. He jammed on the brakes and corrected himself. "Mrs. Roper!"

But Victoria was already out of the car, slamming the door behind her. When she reached to open the door of the office, her husband opened it for her.

He appeared alarmed. "Mother called from the office. Are you all right?"

"I am not all right. The sheriff is at the door. Again."

Victoria pushed her way past him and headed for George's office. The superintendent came out of the adjoining office, saw Victoria, lost his smile, and returned to his office.

George trailed her into his office and closed the door behind them. "Mother said you were upset."

Victoria took one of the visitors' chairs. "Of course I'm upset. I marry you, and you do this to me. How could you?"

"Do what?"

"Oh, George," said Victoria, shifting around in the chair as if she had ants in her bustle, "you know what I mean. Your brother's here to examine the books."

"He's not my brother. He's my cousin."

"Oh, please, do we have to split hairs?"

"My dear, you need not show him the books. You did the right thing."

"But did you do the right thing? Are you going to jail? Must I help you flee as I did Edmund?"

"Pardon me," said George, taking a seat opposite her in the other visitor's chair. "You helped your husband abscond with those people's money?"

"I packed his suitcase. He is, after all, my daughter's

father. I didn't want to see him go to prison. I encouraged him to run."

"You don't see much of him either way."

"His choice." She made a throwaway motion with her hand. "His choice to allow me to divorce him, too, it would appear."

"That was my decision. I couldn't marry you if Edmund didn't allow you to divorce him."

"Your decision?" Victoria sat up in her chair. "What do you mean? I don't understand. You made Edmund divorce me?"

"I don't make anyone do anything. People do what they wish. I only present them with the facts."

"And what facts did you present to Edmund?"

"That if he did not allow you to divorce him, you would never have a life other than the small, cramped one you had at Belles Lodging. I told him you deserved better. Betty Jean deserved better."

"You gave my daughter a job at the mill as an incentive for me to marry you?"

"No. I gave your daughter a job so she wouldn't become . . ." George looked away.

"Become what?"

He turned back to his wife. "Your daughter hangs around the Ottaray Hotel and she's not there to see me."

Victoria leaned forward. "What are you saying, George? What has Betty Jean done?"

"As far as I know, nothing improper, but she's no Catherine Belle."

"What does Katie have to do with this?"

"Catherine lost her family and is making up for lost

time. Ask James Stuart. He's been around both girls. He can tell the difference."

"James Stuart! What has James Stuart done with my daughter?"

"Nothing. He's crazy for Catherine. That's why he's working with Cap'n Billy Sirrine to set up our booth at the new Textile Hall, not because his business brings him to town."

"But Katie's to marry Mark."

"And I married you. I asked Edmund for permission, and he gave it to me. I asked your father for permission, too."

"My father?" Victoria fell back in her chair, stunned.

"I traveled to Ohio to ask his permission. It was before the shooting."

"And?"

"He threw me out of his office."

"Oh, George, I'm so sorry. If you'd only told me—"

"Don't get me wrong. He was all for the marriage—once he heard of your divorce from Edmund."

"But—but you said he threw you out. I don't understand."

"I'm from South Carolina."

"Oh," said Victoria, issuing a weak smile. "That again."

"Yes. That again."

"Father lost his father in the war."

"As did others. Some people can't put things behind them."

"George, I can't put *this* behind me."

"Well," he said, relaxing in his chair, "what is it you

wish to know? You certainly know whether I have any money or not. You keep the company journals."

"That's just it. Do you have . . ."

A knock sounded at the door. It was George's secretary.

"Sorry to bother you, Mr. Roper, but you have visitors."

"My cousin?"

"He insists on seeing you."

"Then send him in." George got to his feet.

Victoria huddled in tight, afraid of this impending storm.

George put a hand on her shoulder. "Let me handle this."

"Oh, George, if you only could." Victoria took a handkerchief from her purse. She looked close to tears.

Samuel Roper charged through the door with his hand out. "George, you old son of a gun. How have you been?"

Victoria was taken aback, but she had seen Samuel operate earlier. He appeared to be a perfect gentleman. Just like Edmund. Just like George.

The two men shook hands, gave each other a hug, and patted each other's backs.

"I suppose congratulations are in order." Samuel took Victoria's hand. "Best wishes to you, Victoria." He gestured at George. "Just watch my cousin. He's a sly devil."

Victoria could only nod.

Samuel turned to the other two men who had followed him through the door. He introduced one man as his attorney, the other as a tax consultant.

"George," said Samuel, "once we conviced your former mother-in-law to allow us to examine your books, we couldn't help but notice that everything is in your name, not Roper and Sons."

Startled, Victoria looked at her new husband.

"And," added Samuel, "after seeing your operation out here along the river, we wondered if you needed to borrow any money."

Twenty-eight

The next time James saw Katie was at Camp Sevier. Just like the Spanish-American War boosters had gone to Washington and lobbied for another cantonment to be established in Greenville. The camp was named in honor of John Sevier who fought at Kings Mountain during the Revolutionary War. National Guard units from North Carolina, South Carolina, and Tennessee reported to Sevier and were formed into the Old Hickory Division. They left for Europe, then other units moved in, were organized, and moved on to Europe as part of the American Expeditionary Force. Sevier occupied almost two thousand acres between Rutherford Road and Wade Hampton Boulevard, and there was so much traffic that a concrete highway had to be built between Sevier and downtown Greenville.

You could watch airplanes soar overhead or watch soldiers line up for the Southern or the Piedmont and Northern railroads. J. E. Sirrine and Fiske-Carter consulted on the job, and army engineers sawed trees, constructed wooden floors, and pitched tents. Hospitals were built last, which was unfortunate, as they were needed sooner rather than later. The Spanish flu moved in almost as quickly as the soldiers.

No one imagined the number of coffins necessary to ship home young men who'd never been jammed into such crowded conditions. And it wasn't only the soldiers who were struck down, but the locals, as the flu leaped the walls of the camp and worked its way through Greenville.

Sometimes the flu had some help.

James shook the reins of his horse and guided his wagon over to where Katie sat sideways in the driver's seat of the Buick, feet on the running board. The vehicle was equipped with a four-cylinder engine rated at forty horsepower and the body style allowed the seating of five, just about perfect for the sisters, their niece, and the occasional hired man.

As usual, dark-haired Katie was surrounded by soldiers. Out of the thousands passing through Sevier, Katie could have her pick, but she remained loyal to Mark's memory and supported the war effort by volunteering in the canteen during the lunch hour. The rest of the day she spent parceling out medicine, scrubbing floors, or playing tennis with recovering patients. But it was the attention of the soldiers, especially the flyers, that drew her to the hangar after her shift ended, and the Buick always attracted some car nut.

James Stuart climbed down from the wagon, leaving a large black man in the driver's box. Across the black man's lap lay a rifle with an eight-round clip; on James's hip rested the Webley automatic pistol. He strolled over to the Buick, and along the way took off his slouch hat, which he used to cover the Webley.

He asked if he could speak to Miss Belle.

Katie looked most appealing. She wore a two-piece gabardine suit: blue trimmed with gold braid and buttons. The coat sported military pockets and a belt. And since her ankles were revealed, Katie had taken to shaving her legs as high as mid-calf.

An officer looked him over, and James observed the officer's name tag and his railroad track insignia. The captain looked smart in his khaki uniform, but James Stuart, in blue jeans and a plaid work shirt, looked like some farmer, his face tanned from long days in the sun. He had just resigned his position with Roper and Sons, one of the reasons he was here.

"May I inquire as to the nature of your business with Miss Belle?" The officer glanced at the wagon. "And why is that Negro inside the wire? Is he your servant?"

"No, sir. From time to time I have to ask Alexander to shoot someone when they try to handle the merchandise."

Katie laughed and stepped down from the car. One of the soldiers gave her a hand. Once on her feet, Katie coughed into a lace-edged handkerchief and dabbed at her eyes. The captain stepped between James and Katie.

"Ronnie," said Katie, taking the officer's arm, "please don't shoot Mr. Stuart. He's a dear friend of the family."

"He isn't polite enough to be a friend of the Belles."

"Well, he's also a friend of the Dukes. You know, the family with the daughter who serves sandwiches at the canteen?"

"That girl has the tastiest mayonnaise. Mother said for me to ask for the recipe."

"Well, let's not disappoint your mother twice in one day."

Leaving the captain with a puzzled look, Katie took James's arm and strolled toward the wagon. Being in this girl's presence was such a tonic, James never noticed he had to slow down for Katie to keep up with him.

"What have you been up to, James?"

"It's not what I've been up to, Allison, but what you've done."

Katie pulled them to a stop. "Why did you call me that?"

"A better question would be: Why did you ride through the Dark Corner? Tell me the truth, Allison, do you remember anything about the day your parents died? I saw three or four horsemen ride away, but that's all. What did you see?"

Katie coughed again, covering her mouth with the handkerchief. "I didn't see anything. Like I told you, I was going over the bridge."

He seized her arm. "Are you telling me the truth? That's not the Allison McKelvey I know, taunting those riders."

"Take your hand off me!" Katie backed away, almost stumbling and dropping her handkerchief. "You can't tell me what to do."

James followed her, stepping forward, not releasing

his hold. "With our testimonies, there's a slight, and I mean a slight possibility, that the two remaining Laughlins might, and I say might, be sent to prison for your family's deaths."

"Why only two?"

He gripped her by both arms now. "Because you killed one of them where your family's carriage went off the bridge. How many more people have to die?"

"He should've been a better rider."

Startled, James considered slapping some sense into her. He had no idea why this girl could get under his skin so deeply. Evidently, he did not have the same effect on her.

"Allison," said James, releasing her arms, "this is James you're talking to, not some old maid."

The captain had seen enough and started in their direction.

Katie folded her arms across her chest, leaned back, and regarded him. "I wanted to visit my family, is that so awful?"

"Actions have consequences."

She waved him off. "Oh, don't reheat that old chestnut."

"I won't always be there to protect you. I'm joining up, and you've got to promise—"

"Miss Belle," said the captain, "I must insist on asking you if this man is troubling you. I can have him thrown off base if necessary."

"You see, James, I have friends, too."

James snorted. "And that's why women are always disappointed in their men." To the black man in the wagon, he said, "Alexander, empty that rifle and toss it to the officer."

Alexander removed the clip and cleared the chamber, popping the seated round free. The rifle flew in the captain's direction. He fielded it neatly.

He hefted the weapon. "What's this?"

"The first mass-produced semiautomatic rifle made in America. John Garand developed it at the Springfield Armory."

The captain looked up from examining the weapon. "How do you come by it?"

"John's a friend of mine. He asked me to field test it."

"What field? Where would you test such a weapon?"

"Where are you from, Captain?"

"Chicago."

"Well, we don't have any cities as large as Chicago, but we have plenty of farms."

"Would you mind if I tried it?" asked the captain, turning the weapon over in his hands. "We have a rather decent range here at Sevier."

Turning to the wagon again, James called out, "Alexander, accompany the officer to the range, and if he has any problem with the Garand, lend him a hand."

"The Negro can handle this weapon?" The surprise showed on the captain's face. Neither man noticed Katie coughing.

"Yes, sir. He can."

The captain cleared the action for himself. "I wouldn't be surprised if the Garand—is that how you pronounce it?"

"Don't worry, sir. I don't think John's had anyone pronounce his name the same way twice."

"Well, thank you, Mr. Stuart." He nodded to Katie,

and before he had walked ten yards he was surrounded by soldiers inquiring about this new weapon.

Katie dabbed at her mouth. "Touché, James."

"Your success in the Dark Corner has gone to your head. I have it on good authority that a Spartanburg County deputy has been looking for you. I believe he was going to call it a day, then you pulled this fool stunt."

"He must not be much of a deputy if he can't find me."

"I really don't think he's tried, but now, with the death of Andrew, he might start looking again."

Katie tried to say something, but James cut her off.

"I read your article about Sevier in *McCall's*. Why can't you concentrate on your writing instead of trying to get yourself killed?"

Katie's chin jutted out. "I do what I wish, thank you very much, and my aunts support me."

"But must you fly all over the state?"

Katie wiped her nose. "Men live as they please, why not women?" She paused for another cough.

"Katie, are you all right?"

But the young woman steamed along, ignoring his concern. "You men may not allow us the right to vote—"

"I came here to ask you to stop taking these wild chances because Mark's been found. He's on his way home."

Katie's legs weakened and she reached out. James took her in his arms, and she coughed in his face.

"Mark's . . . alive? You found him?"

"Our German agent found him in an Austrian hospital. He's shell-shocked, but physically fine."

"Alive? Mark's alive?"

"He'll be home in a few weeks. I received a telegram while I was on the road."

"Oh, James, can this possibly be true?"

He had her in his arms now and for the first time James noticed the redness around her eyes. Her nose ran.

To a passing soldier, he said, "Bring this woman some water."

"No, no," said Katie, gripping his shoulder and trying to stand on her own. "I must tell everyone Mark's all right."

James scooped her up in his arms. Katie had gone limp and her eyes had trouble focusing. A rash covered her face and neck, something James had initially attributed to her anger.

"Mark's family already knows; so do your aunts. It was you who was hard to find, until I remembered all the flying."

She smiled up at him. "You always know the right thing to do." And her eyes rolled back in her head and she was gone.

Twenty-nine

The soldier arrived with the water, but sprinkling it on Katie's face did not revive her long. As soon as she realized where she was and remembered what James had told her, she swooned again. James scooped her up and rushed her over to the Buick—where an argument broke out among several soldiers over whether the girl would be better off in the camp hospital or at home. James said little, but when he tried to take the wheel, a soldier called for an MP.

The soldier who requested the MP hadn't seen the handover of the Garand rifle to his captain or the number of soldiers who followed the officer to the firing range. His head had been under the hood of the touring car—the latest model Buick—and he wasn't pleased to have James order him to put down the hood and move away from the car.

The sergeant of the guard shouted, "Out of the car, sir!"

The sergeant of the guard and his men were always

stationed near the vehicle because Katie drew men like flies to honey.

"I'm trying to get this girl to a doctor."

"It's not his vehicle, Sarge," insisted the car nut.

"Sir, dismount from the vehicle."

James glanced at Katie. She seemed to be breathing properly, even able to cough in her state of unconsciousness. He killed the engine, and as he climbed out of the Buick the sergeant of the guard noticed Stuart was armed.

The sergeant drew his weapon, a .45-caliber that could blow a hole though James as large as a baseball. "Hands up, sir!"

The rifles of the MPs swung around on him.

James sighed, raised his hands, and soon found himself in the stockade with no one particularly interested in his queries about the condition of the camp mascot. Well, the camp mascot after the Duke girl and her mother's mayonnaise.

Katie regained consciousness in the hospital, sat up, and put her feet over the side of the cot. Her head ached, but she remembered James had said Mark was on his way home. She must go home and prepare for Mark's homecoming.

And where *was* James?

Never around when you needed him!

She coughed, and a nurse rushed to her side. "Careful, we have enough people in here as it is."

Once on her feet, Katie looked down the rows and rows of beds, patients coughing under sheer fabric tents.

"What's . . . what's wrong with them?"

"Measles, it would appear. A few of them have pneumonia or the flu. Have you had measles?"

Katie had not. She'd been raised in the isolation of the Dark Corner where snakebite or a broken limb were more likely.

The nurse peeled back Katie's collar, saw the splotches, and hastily covered them.

"You need to go home. Tell your family you've contracted the measles. They can treat you far better than we can. Remain in isolation or you risk the chance of infecting others."

The nurse gestured down the row of fabric tents. "Soon, there won't be enough beds to go round. If I release you, Katie, you'll go straight home?" insisted the nurse.

"Yes, of course."

Katie didn't care to be quarantined. She had to find her car and return to Greenville to make sure all was well for Mark's homecoming. Driving home, Katie tried to remember what James had said about Mark's condition but simply couldn't do it. Her head ached and occasionally she couldn't stop coughing.

That didn't matter. She'd go to Mark's house and help his mother prepare for her son's homecoming. That'd get the old lady out of her sickbed.

Two days after being arrested, Alexander was released from the outhouse where he'd been held prisoner. A black man couldn't be held in the same facilities with white men, and the outhouse was the only thing available. Overhearing the guards talk, he learned that Stuart was in the stockade. Hands cuffed, Alexander allowed himself to be turned over to the county sheriff.

"This way," said the deputy, gesturing Alexander to the rear of a truck. "Lord, boy, but you smell."

As the doors of the truck closed behind him, and Alexander sat chained to his seat, he puzzled as to what to do. The wagon and the guns were gone, and probably the sugar, too. He and Stuart were locked up, possibly facing a rope. What could he do that some white man had not already tried?

Arriving at the county lockup, he asked, "Has anyone seen my fiddle?"

Nobody had, nor did anyone care when Alexander bragged that he was the best fiddle player in the state.

"Never heard of you, boy," said one of the deputies.

"I'm from Charleston."

"You really think you're the best?"

Alexander grinned. The secret to cracking a Carolina boy was to challenge him to a contest. It appeared most white boys suffered from what was called an inferiority complex. Alexander had heard white men discussing this malady and had asked Stuart what the phrase meant. Damn silly idea, if you asked him.

The following day, the deputy asked, "Where's this fiddle of yours, boy? Dean would like to give you a go."

"One of the Belle sisters has it. I don't know which one."

The deputy regarded the black man through the bars.

"All I've got to do is go over to Belles Lodging and they'll have your fiddle and you'll give it a go with Dean?"

"Yes, sir. Just ask for Miss Katie Belle."

"And you have the money to back any wager."

"My money's inside the fiddle, and the fiddle's inside the case. Like I said, ask the Belles."

Later in the day Mary Kate appeared at the county lockup and was taken back to see Alexander. She had no fiddle and told the black man just that.

Alexander shook his head. "Seems like things go from worse to worser. How is Miss Katie?"

"She has the measles. Why are you in jail?"

"Loitering at a federal facility is the charge," said the deputy.

"Well, I think I can pay that fine so I can get my colored boy back to work. And James Stuart . . . where's he?"

They found Stuart in the stockade, surrounded by men covered with red splotches and coughing their heads off.

To the sergeant of the guard, Mary Kate said, "I'm taking this man home."

"Miss, you're welcome to him, but I'll need some paperwork."

"Whom do I see?"

"The captain's down with the flu, so I really don't know what to tell you."

Mary Kate had to go up the chain of command all the way to the commanding officer; there were that many people on sick call. Alexander waited outside while Mary Kate charged into the CO's office and leveled her accusation.

"Sir, one of your captains is in possession of a Garand rifle belonging to a friend of my family and I've come to retrieve it."

The CO stood up behind his desk. "Pardon me, Miss Belle, but what's a Garand rifle?"

The rifle was returned, as was the Webley automatic pistol, but the horse and wagon were gone for good.

"You don't leave a wagon unattended around a bunch of soldiers," said James, starting the Buick. "You probably couldn't even find an axle if you looked for it."

"The horse?" asked Alexander.

"Probably sold off-post."

"Can you file a claim with Washington?" asked Mary Kate.

"Washington's in chaos at the moment. I might hear from them by the time Wilson's elected to a third term." As he drove the three of them out of the gate, he asked, "How's Katie?"

"Came home two days ago all excited about Mark's return. Yesterday we put her to bed. She's in the spare room in the attic across from Johnny."

"Well, I hope Uncle John has had the measles."

"Johnny had everything while locked up in that Yankee prison camp. Nothing can touch John. James, you were locked in the stockade with all those soldiers. Why haven't you come down with the measles?"

"Alexander and I are from Charleston. When

Alexander and I grew up, livestock still roamed the streets and the water wasn't safe to drink. I was more worried about contracting pneumonia. There's no immunization against pneumonia."

"Katie said you had something to do with finding Mark."

James shook his head as he turned out on the concrete highway that would lead into town. "The family broker in Germany made the identification."

"Don't tell me your company still does business with the Germans."

"My family severed our relationship when the *Lusitania* went down. Our broker's the one who wants to maintain the relationship, and it looks like Katie's reaping the benefits."

Mary Kate let this go, instead saying, "Katie told us there's something wrong with Mark."

"He's shell-shocked and I have no idea how long it will take for him to recover."

"Shell-shocked?"

"Remember those Confederates who returned from the war jumpy and anxious?"

"I remember. People said they'd lost their nerve."

"They weren't cowards. Shell-shocked soldiers suffer fatigue and indecision. They can't pick one activity over another. Katie will need the patience of Job to deal with Mark."

Thirty

James Stuart sat in a chair by Katie's bed in the spare room in the attic. From time to time one of her aunts looked in, and twice the doctor had stopped by. Because John Belle made little noise across the hall, James suspected that Uncle John was very sick. Maybe even dead.

"And guess who signed my license?" asked Katie, breaking out of her delirium. She repeated the story about Herbert Mitchum teaching her to fly. "Orville Wright signed my aviator's license. Isn't that amazing?"

James smiled.

Katie coughed. "Have I told you this story before?"

"Of course not."

She took his hand and tried to squeeze it. The hand failed to apply much pressure. "You're a very patient man, James."

"I'm jealous. You have all those beaus."

In her delirium, Katie had told him everything about

her learning how to fly, and James vowed that if he ever ran into Herbert Mitchum he would beat the flyer within an inch of his life. The man had no honor. On the positive side, Katie had fewer nightmares about falling off . . . something . . . somewhere.

Margaret said the secret to ending Katie's nightmares was reading, so as soon as Katie's fever broke, James carried a stack of books upstairs, though the two young people differed over reading material.

Katie took his hand and tried to squeeze it. "We must find you a girlfriend."

"I already have one, and she keeps me plenty busy."

"Not me, silly. What about Betty Jean?"

"Not my type."

James didn't tell Katie that Betty Jean had run off with a young man, that the steady job at the Saluda River Mill had not been enough to hold her to Greenville. She was too much like her father, a risk-taker and a rambler.

Even in this delirium Katie revealed information that made James wince, even sometimes drove him from the room.

Katie imagined Betty Jean had stopped by and spent the afternoon with her.

"Daddy won't take me with him. I think he came back to see if my mother had any money since she's married to Mr. Roper."

"Your father's in Greenville?"

"Slipped into town to see me. Gave me a few bucks not to tell my mother. I pleaded with him to let me go

along, but he was headed to South America. He made me promise not to tell, so you can't."

"South America? How exotic."

Betty Jean laughed. "Everyone thought you were the naughty girl, but all along it was me. Katie, you must learn to keep your head down when you're only thinking about being wicked."

"What about your mother's family in Columbus?"

"Nobody knows us in Ohio. I wish I'd lost my family like you. Then I could start anew."

"No, no. Don't wish that on anyone."

After a pause, Betty Jane confided that Gerald wanted her to run off with him.

Remembering Herbert Mitchum trapping her in that cotton field in Laurens County, Katie said, "Gerald just wants you."

"He's already had that."

Katie could not believe what she'd just heard. "You're funning me."

Betty Jean leaned toward the bed. "I gave it to him to find out if he really loved me or if it was just that."

"Oh, my Lord!" Katie's hand rose to her throat.

Betty Jean smiled slyly. "Don't you want to know what it's like? I've done it more than once."

"Yes," said Katie, glancing at the bedroom door, which, for some reason, appeared to be more like the spare room in the attic, not the room she shared with the old maids. "But first close the door."

"I'm so happy Mark's home," said Katie, during one of her more lucid days. "I just wish you could be this happy."

"I am. I love reading out loud."

Katie tried to reach over and hit him but didn't have the strength. Just raising her arm caused her to gag. After clearing her throat, she said, "You're just saying that."

"Oh, no, your aunts are thrilled," said James, holding a glass of water so that Katie could drink from it to stop the coughing. "They don't have a moment's worry about you."

Katie sipped from the glass and cleared her throat. "You make me sound like a real bother."

"Good-looking women are never a bother."

Katie fingered her matted-down hair. "I need my hair washed. Can you send for the hairdresser?"

"You stay right there and you'll be fine. I'll find a book I haven't read yet."

While James sorted through the stack, Katie said, "I remember you saying you were joining up."

"Probably just your delirium talking."

"Please don't be that way, James. Sometimes it's hard to know whether I'm here or gone again."

James leaned over and wiped away the tears with a cloth handkerchief. "The army learned I had all sorts of diseases while growing up, so I'm holding down your position at the hospital until you've recovered." And evenings, he read Jane Austen with the door of the spare room open. And puzzled over why women fell for these brooding, sophisticated, and educated men detached from society. It was cause enough for Katie's boyfriend to keep his distance upon arriving next week. Mark had forgotten how to act Byronic.

"A gun salesman emptying bedpans?" asked Katie, amused.

"We're not to question the mysterious workings of the United States Army."

"What about the Ropers?"

"George goes house to house in the village making sure everyone's windows are open and those who are sick sleep in a room of their own. Victoria's working at the community center. It's lined with beds with linen canopies."

"Why open windows?"

James pointed at the dormer window over Katie's bed. It, too, was open and part of the slanted ceilings on the third floor.

"If people are secluded in their own fabric tents in hospitals, doctors must believe the flu is spread by groups. So maybe by having your own room and having the windows open, there's less chance the flu will be spread. Church services have been canceled, there're no moving pictures, no school being held. Seems to be working. The deaths are down at Saluda Mill."

He held up a book. "What about Sherlock Holmes tonight?"

"You can't learn anything from two cantankerous old men."

"The men you deride learned to live together, and they were as different as night and day."

"If you call that living. When Sherlock's not on a case, he's filling his arm with cocaine."

"Can you imagine anyone being called 'Sherlock'? What a name."

"Irene Adler. Irene would call Holmes 'Sherlock.'" Katie forced a smile. "The only person to outsmart Holmes was a woman."

James shuffled through the books. Behind his chair stood a stack of envelopes filled with Katie's writings. Up to now the sick girl had not asked for them. "How about *Tarzan of the Apes?* It has a love story."

"Where the hero rescues the maiden in distress—a bit obsolete in the modern day. Heard anything from Mark?"

"Sorry, Katie, but they're not going to allow him to visit until you're well enough to see him."

"I'm not infectious."

James said nothing.

She regarded him. "They're waiting for the next shoe to drop, aren't they?"

James remained silent.

"I don't have to contract pneumonia."

James gestured at the door. "Well, if you do, you'll find me sitting in the hallway."

Katie took his hand. "James, promise me you'll be here when I wake up."

"Oh, yes," said James with a laugh. "It appears I can't help myself."

The next time Katie woke, her chest ached and she had difficulty breathing, And she was hot. Very hot. James had fallen asleep in the chair across the hall from the open door, but when Katie cleared her throat, the sound jolted him into action.

Seeing Katie trying to throw off the sheet, James leaped from his chair and raced into her room, tying a handkerchief over his nose and mouth.

"No, no." He held her by the shoulder and into the bed. "Lie down, Katie. Don't aggravated yourself. You don't want to start coughing again."

Startled by his sudden appearance, the sick girl instantly understood her condition and lay back in her bed, the sheet bunched at her feet. "But I'm hot."

"Better hot than this." He held up a dried bloody cloth.

"Me?"

James only nodded, then wet a cloth from a bucket by the bed and gently washed her face. Finished, he replaced the dry cloth on her forehead with a damp one.

"Am I dying?" she asked in a hoarse whisper.

"Just feverish. And you want to cough."

"I wish I was dead. I'm so hot. I'm burning up."

"The world's a much more exciting place with you around. Just think of all the girls you've inspired."

It was a long moment before Katie made the connection. "When's . . . when's the next march?"

"What does it matter? You'll be in bed."

"It's not fair," she said, frowning. "You should give us the vote."

"And give up our powers over you women?"

"You've never . . ." She coughed, and when she brought down the cloth, James was relieved to see it contained no blood. "You men have never had power . . . over us."

James grinned. What could he say?

Katie rambled on and on about places she had traveled. After calling in her story to the *Piedmont*, she always took time to speak to the issue of women's suffrage, then hopped into her plane for the return flight home.

She rolled her head away. "I can't believe I'm letting you see me like this. I'm a mess."

James dropped the dry cloth into the bucket. "Never once since I've know you have I gotten the idea that you were trying to impress me. That's why I'm here instead of Mark. You're wearing no makeup."

Katie became indignant, but when she tried to speak, the pain in her chest crushed her words. "I've always . . . I've always been true . . . to Mark."

"Of that, there's no doubt, and he can't wait to see you. Comes all the way home from Europe and you're sick as a dog."

She labored to get out: "My hair? My hair has to . . . has to look good for Mark."

"You're absolutely stunning." James didn't tell her that her hair was growing out blond, and that they'd have to dye it before Mark could see her.

"Liar." She coughed. "It itches."

"That's the pneumonia talking."

She set her jaw. "Two down . . . and the flu to go."

He took her hand and squeezed it. "Just concentrate on Mark, Katie. Always think of Mark and you'll be fine."

"And Mark?"

"There's sickness at his house, but everyone's fighting it. Mark had the flu while in Germany. When he arrives home, he'll be immune."

"And the Old Maids' Club?"

"Just concentrate on getting well."

She coughed. "Who?"

It was a moment before he said, "Mary Kate's come down with pneumonia. Margaret's sitting with her."

"She got it from me, didn't she?" Tears appeared in her eyes and she turned away. The cloth slid from her forehead. "I've brought nothing but misery to this family."

"Katie, don't say that."

"I thought I was so special, you know, surviving the fall into the river and the death of my family." She began to cry. "I tried very hard."

James replaced the cloth on her forehead once she stopped thrashing around. "Everyone's proud of your accomplishments."

She looked up from under the cloth. "Even Aunt Helen?"

"Especially Helen. Over breakfast this morning, she told me she could never have imagined all you would accomplish after the Old Maids' Club voted to suspend your chores."

"Split vote, I'd imagine."

"What does it matter? You've won over the most hard-hearted of three."

In a moment, she asked, "Did I tell you about the novel I'm writing?"

"The one featuring Mary Kate—yes. Set during the Civil War in Laurens County." James glanced at the stacks of typewritten pages in envelopes. "But do you really think people will want to read about such a manipulative character?"

"She's in love . . ." Katie struggled to get out, ". . . with her sister's beau . . . all's fair in . . ."

When James looked again, Katie was gone.

And once again, James studied her chest and the necklace with Mark's class ring. Only when Katie's chest began to rise and fall did he pull the sheet up over her and return to his chair in the attic hallway. Instantly, he fell asleep.

Margaret Belle climbed the stairs with another tray. It wasn't just the stair-climbing, but this whole influenza business taking its toll. Her face was lined with worry, her once luxurious black hair now streaked with gray. She turned to the spare room where the door stood open and James had set a fan so it would pull air from the bedroom and push it through the dormer window overhead.

James's chair remained in the hallway, but Margaret found the young man kneeling by Katie's bed, holding her hand, a handkerchief wrapped around the lower part of his face.

Margaret stood there for the longest, then cleared her throat. Startled, James dropped Katie's hand, got to his feet, and came to the door.

"Why don't you tell her, James?"

He pulled the handkerchief down around his neck. "I . . . I don't know what you mean."

"That you've been in love with her from the first day you pulled her from that river."

James looked at the sleeping woman with the half black, half blond hair. "It's not something we can count on."

"Count on?"

"We have to give Katie something to hang onto, and that's Mark."

Margaret shook her head and turned away. "Well, we can always count on you to do the right thing, even if it's not right for you. I'll get the hair coloring. When Mark comes to visit, Katie's hair must be completely black."

The deputy from Spartanburg County arrived at Belles Lodging with his cousin in tow and asked to see Allison McKelvey.

Robert Patton answered the door. He didn't know who Allison McKelvey was. Margaret, however, playing the upright piano in the parlor, heard the pull bell and joined them at the door.

"I'll handle this, Robert." Margaret could see the deputy's truck at the curb. "What can I do for you, Officer?"

The deputy gestured at the man beside him, an ashen-faced man wearing a cowboy hat with a rattlesnake head at the front. "This is my cousin, Cleve Laughlin. He's here to see your niece."

Laughlin did not look good. He appeared pale and weak with a nervous tic, hardly able to stand.

Cleve saw her evaluating him. "I've got the pneumonia, Miss Belle. My cousins are dead, and I don't think I'll last the week, so I asked the deputy to bring me to see Allison."

"I don't think we have anyone in this house by that name."

"Miss Belle, I want to apologize for the trouble we've caused. I don't want to go to my grave with that on my conscience."

"Perhaps you should've thought about that before you starting feuding."

"I don't really know what the feud was about,

something a McKelvey did to a Laughlin three generations ago."

"Or a Laughlin did to a McKelvey."

"Yeah," said Cleve, smiling. "It could've been that way."

"Miss Belle," said the deputy, "we're not here to cause any fuss. Cleve wants Allison to know the feud dies with him."

Laughlin gave her a wan smile. "Which I don't think'll be much longer."

"My niece is on her deathbed. I'll give her the message."

Margaret tried to close the door, but the deputy put a foot inside. "Please, Miss Belle. People need to end this."

"She may not even be conscious."

The deputy gestured at the rockers on the wraparound porch. "We'll wait out here."

"No guns allowed in this house."

The deputy opened his jacket so the Belle woman could see his empty belt. "Then you and I have something in common."

Margaret watched the deputy assist his cousin over to a rocker and take a seat. It was true what the deputy said: Neither man carried any weapon.

Margaret stepped out on the porch. "I'm going to have to convince Katie's fiancé to allow you to see her."

"Very well, Miss Belle," said the deputy. "If you have any trouble, send him to see me. I'm a pretty good talker myself." He touched his hip before sitting down. "I have to be."

A few minutes later, Mark opened the door, stepped outside, and introduced himself.

The two men got up from their rockers, quite an effort for Cleve. "Appreciate you doing this," he said to Mark.

"I'm going home." The tall, thin young man appeared anxious, unsure of himself. "She's not got long to live, and I've done my best."

The deputy wasn't impressed with Allison's choice of men. He nodded his good-bye.

"Sorry about this," said Cleve.

Mark started down the steps, then jerked back in their direction. "What? What?"

"We're sorry about your fiancée's illness," said the deputy.

"Fiancée? I'm not engaged to anyone. I'm just visiting."

Down the stairs Mark went, walking quickly as if someone or something pursued him, something or someone only he could see. The men on the porch watched him stop at the curb and look in both directions. Matter of fact, Mark looked in both directions twice.

"Jumpy fellow," said the deputy. "Hard to believe the Bloomer Babe had any interest in him."

"I remember him from the roadhouse," said Cleve, "before he went overseas. He wasn't like that."

"Everybody changes when they go off to war."

The door opened behind them and a middle-aged man stepped out on the porch. "You here to see Katie?"

The two men nodded.

The middle-aged man glanced at the snakehead on the hat. "I don't know what your business is, but I told Margaret I'd come down and read you the riot act."

"You the fiancé?" asked the deputy.

"I'm the doctor. This girl comes and goes, and one time she's not coming back. Can you make it quick?"

Cleve stepped toward the door. "I can try, but quick hasn't been my strong suit the last few days."

"Flu?" asked the doctor.

"Pneumonia."

The doctor shook his head. "The girl has influenza. Best you didn't see her at all."

"Can I infect her?" asked Cleve.

"No, but she can kill you."

Cleve considered this. "Seems about right."

The doctor held open the door, and the deputy gave his cousin a hand over the stoop. Both men saw James Stuart standing at the foot of the stairs, his hand on the butt of the Webley.

Cleve nodded. "I knew there was a connection."

"You're damned right. I pulled her from the river the day you and your cousins ran her family's carriage off that bridge."

"It was an accident." Cleve glanced at the deputy. "We were just funning. It got out of hand."

"I thought no weapons were allowed in this house," said the deputy, studying the Webley.

"And that's what you get for listening to an old maid," said James. "Hands over your head!"

The phone on the pedestal table rang, and a woman in black rushed from the parlor and took the call. She listened, nodded, and after hanging up, reported another death at Corbett Home.

Cleve coughed instead of hoisting his hands over his head. "I don't know . . . if I can . . ."

James didn't budge. "I'll frisk you after you hit the floor."

"Look," said the doctor, watching the woman dressed in black return to the parlor. "I've lost another one over at Corbett so I don't need all this fussing. You'll upset my patient."

"Don't worry, Doc," said James, touching the Webley. "They'll come along peacefully." He grinned at Cleve. "It's three floors. Think you can make it?"

Cleve's face turned grim. "I got to."

Laughlin didn't collapse, but he did have to be assisted to the third-floor landing by both James and the deputy. Once Cleve reached the third floor, he stood at the head of the stairs, swaying back and forth and coughing. He simply couldn't stop coughing. The doctor offered him some water, and that helped.

"You know," said the deputy, trying to catch his breath, "this is damned ridiculous."

"Don't you . . . know it," coughed Cleve.

Both Helen and Margaret stood in the third-floor room, the door to Uncle Johnny's room open and John's room empty. Cleve staggered into the spare room, past the fan, and over to the bed. He nodded to Robert Patton and Eugene, took off his hat, and sat in the chair beside Katie's bed. On a small table under a sloping ceiling sat the doctor's black bag.

"Know who I am?" he asked the girl.

Katie glanced at the snakehead. "I've seen your hat before . . . when I was out riding."

"Nice horse . . . that mustang. You're quite the rider."

"Or I'd be dead . . . by your hand or your cousins'."

"My cousins are dead. That's why I'm here."

Tears welled up in Katie's eyes. She rolled her head over on the pillow and stared at the wall. It was an effort to speak, and no matter whether the dormer window was open or not, she sweated under a single sheet. Still, the hair and filth did not bother her, no, not this afternoon. Until this afternoon, she hadn't cared whether she lived or died. Then Mark had arrived, looking shaken and disoriented, and Katie had become determined to live—if only for Mark. Mark needed her.

"Look," said Cleve, glancing at those standing around Katie's bed, "I'm here to apologize . . . for all the trouble my family's caused you." He coughed.

"Good," said James. "Get right to the point."

Cleve looked up at him. "After climbing those stairs, that's . . . all I'm able to do."

Katie looked from one face to another. "If he's here, does this mean I'm dying?"

Everyone shook their head.

"No, honey," said Cleve, "you're too pretty to die."

"So were my parents."

"Katie!" said Helen.

"Katie," said Margaret, "Mr. Laughlin's here to apologize."

Again, Katie turned her head away from Laughlin.

"Hey," said Cleve, straightening up, "I deserve anything she gives me."

"Katie," said James, "if it'll make you feel any better, I'll let you use the Webley."

Everyone in the attic room cut their eyes in James's

direction. The two old maids said, "James!"

Katie smiled at him. "You always know the right words." Tears started down her cheeks. "That's why Mark came over, isn't it? I'm dying, aren't I?"

Margaret handed the girl her handkerchief. Neither old maid said anything. Katie dabbed at her eyes.

"Hey," said the doctor, rolling off the door, "don't be upsetting my patient."

"Well," said Cleve, "I'd best be going,"

He tried to get to his feet but couldn't do it without assistance from the deputy and James Stuart.

"No," said Katie, after clearing her throat. "Let him sit a while. After all, he did climb all those stairs."

Thirty-one

A few weeks later, a soldier at Sevier opened his eyes, saw the girl hovering over him, and asked, "Are you an angel?"

"You may think so," said Katie, smiling at the man in the hospital bed. She held a bucket and ladle for passing out medicine. "The doctor thinks you're going to make it."

Overnight, the man's fever had broken, and it pleased Katie no end. She didn't want another corpse hauled out of here.

Every day, caskets were stacked like cordwood at the gates of Camp Sevier and hauled to the West Washington station or the Augusta Street depot for shipment home to the dead man's relatives. Locals were buried in Springwood Cemetery. Mary Kate had been buried there last month in a casket with a sack of Hershey's kisses, and it had nearly torn apart the Old Maids' Club. Mary Kate had been the peacemaker. Now there was none.

Eugene said Katie was the new peacemaker. Eugene had been left the snakehead cowboy hat by Cleve Laughlin, who spent his last days in Uncle John's room at the request of the Belle sisters upon learning he had no woman to care for him.

"Seems about right," muttered Helen.

Before he died, Cleve had left all his property to Catherine Belle, and after "Miss Jim" Perry came to the attic to draft his will, Cleve had said, "That's in case Allison ever wants to return to the Dark Corner."

Katie was also the buffer when Mark's father raged at him for being jumpy and anxious. Why couldn't he find a job and stop hanging around the house? That's what men do! They work!

Katie made it clear that she would become engaged if Mark asked, even go through with the wedding if she must.

Her aunts had been horrified. Marriage to a man who refused to remember his love for you was worse than becoming a member of an old maids' club.

"After all we sacrificed." Helen shook her head.

"She owes us nothing," said Margaret. "It's her life."

"Well," finished Helen, "best she become an old maid than be trapped in a loveless marriage."

The doctor had read up on Mark's condition. Mark wasn't a scaredy-cat. He had simply repressed what had happened to him overseas, along with his feelings for Katie.

Katie threw herself into her work at Camp Sevier, well, at least a couple of hours a day until she completely recovered. She also encouraged James to spend more time with Mark. She could always count on James.

"I need to find that man a girlfriend," said Katie, one morning while rolling biscuits.

"I have a candidate," said Helen, slicing the bacon once again. "You!"

Katie laughed. "Oh, James and I don't think that way about each other."

"How would you know?" asked Margaret, gathering up the napkins and silverware for the breakfast table.

Katie stopped rolling the biscuits. "That's the most preposterous thing I've ever heard. I'll admit that I was infatuated with him at one time. It's only natural. He did pull me from that river."

Helen inclined her head at their niece. "More big words to avoid making difficult decisions."

Margaret smiled as she left the kitchen with the tray of silverware and cloth napkins. "There was a time when you'd be pleased to hear Catherine use such language. At least it's not slang."

Katie turned to Helen. "What's gotten into you?"

"A better question," said Helen, eyeballing her cut on the bacon with her knife, "would be: What's gotten into you?"

"What ever do you mean? I just recovered from the measles, pneumonia, and the Spanish flu."

"Uh-huh. First time I've heard you use an excuse for not getting something done."

"That's slang."

"Don't change the subject."

Katie brushed off her hands. "What is the subject?"

"The attractiveness of James Stuart as a beau."

"I said I'd find him a girlfriend."

"Right, Emma. You do just that."

Katie frowned. "First it's 'Allison,' then 'Catherine,' and now 'Emma.' Aunt Helen, don't tell me you've been reading Jane Austen."

Margaret, who'd been listening in the hallway, stuck her head in the kitchen. "Don't change the subject."

When they received word that John's wife and her mother had died from the flu, Helen asked Katie to take the intercity trolley to Spartanburg and attend the funerals in their stead. Doing so was more than Helen was willing to do, and at that moment it was touch and go for Margaret, who also had the flu. Robert Patton spent most of his time outside the master bedroom door and on his knees, praying.

When Katie returned with confirmation that Theresa and her mother had indeed perished from the flu, Mary Kate nodded from her deathbed. "Time to let Johnny go, too."

She explained that John Belle had died more than twenty years before, a secret held by the sisters because the house would be inherited by Theresa Belle, not John's siblings. When John died, the sisters had buried their brother in the garden behind the house, and the Old Maids' Club took special pride in fooling their next-door neighbor, Mrs. Dutton.

With the death of Theresa and her mother, Margaret and Helen Belle took to the streets during the next Indian summer's rally to demand the right to vote. Katie was happy to have her aunts marching beside her.

"It's been a long time coming."

"Suffrage has always put a young woman's face on the movement," said Helen. "The leadership never wanted the movement to be known as a bunch of cranky old women."

"So, we've missed nothing," said Margaret, as the four of them, including Mrs. George Roper, strolled under a canopy of autumn leaves in the direction of the new courthouse being built beside Mansion House Hotel.

Eudora Ramsay, who had returned from New York, led a group of young women from Greenville Woman's College that swarmed down Laurens Street. All wore ribbons of purple, white, and gold. At the intersection of Laurens, West Coffee, and Buncombe streets, commonly called Five Points, Eudora pulled Margaret Belle aside to inquire as to the health of her niece.

"Good, good, good," said Margaret enthusiastically.

"I was so worried, but I knew Katie was in good hands."

Margaret laughed. "Oh, Eudora, you just don't know."

Clerks poured out of the rear entrance of Meyers-Arnold, girls left boyfriends at the soda fountain adjoining the drug store, and out-of-towners left husbands at the Hotel Virginia to join the march. Mechanics with greasy hands and cigarettes dangling from their mouths left their repairs and gaped at the number of women headed for the new assembly point on Main, the new courthouse.

Before they reached the construction site, Katie was surrounded by young women and girls who wished to march beside the only woman in the state who reported for a newspaper, could ride like a man, and fly an airplane. Rumor was Katie would soon go to Europe to cover the war. Girls gripped Katie's hands, photographs were snapped with Brownie cameras, and autographs were given. It was a grand time to be a woman, if you didn't mind not having the right to vote.

In front of the courthouse, Katie hugged Maud Younger, who would later speak at the Colonial Theatre. Younger, an independently wealthy socialite, had worked in New York as a waitress, then returned to California to organize San Francisco's first waitress union. Katie, the conference's keynote speaker, would precede Younger and speak on "Carolina Girls: Life Beyond the Finish Line of Suffrage."

Helen Vaughan, chairwoman of the state party, inquired as to how Katie felt. "I heard you're spending more and more time at Sevier since your recovery."

The seventeen-year-old threw out her arms to acknowledge the throng, who responded with another cheer. A few steps away, "Miss Jim" Perry and Ellen Perry smiled. This was one girl who wouldn't have to leave South Carolina to achieve what she wanted.

Katie gave the state party chair a big hug. "I could collapse any moment, Mrs. Vaughan, but not until the end of such a splendid day." Katie threw her arms around her aunts and hugged them tightly. "I just wish Mary Kate could've been here."

"Oh," said Margaret, glancing skyward, "she is."

As they marched down Main Street, shoulder-to-shoulder, Victoria Roper pointed out two young men leaning against a telephone pole. Katie broke ranks with the others and fought her way through the crowd to where the young men stood.

"Thanks for coming."

James rolled off the telephone pole, noting that Katie wore her mother's necklace but this time with no class ring. "Well, Mark needed to stretch his legs anyway."

Katie smiled at Mark, but took James's arm and tried to pull him off the curb. The Charlestonian resisted.

"Come march with us, James. If there's a man who's done more for women in the upstate, I don't know who he'd be."

James glanced down a street filled with marching women, chanting women, angry women. Merchants stood at doors, arms crossed; soldiers from Sevier appeared stunned, even frightened. They would rather face the Germans than this crowd.

"Not me. I have to do business in this town."

"Well, you'll never do business with me again if you don't join this march."

James glanced at Mark, who looked away.

When James returned his attention to the girl, hope flared in his eyes. "And what business would that be, Miss Belle? As long as I've known you, you've always been spoken for."

Katie looped her arm in James's and forced him to join the march for women's rights. "Is that something you picked up in the Dark Corner? You know you can't believe everything you hear about that place."

James laughed as they marched along, arm in arm. "And *what* can I believe, Miss Belle?"

"That there's a new kind of woman coming along, and if they're anything like me, most of them can figure out just about everything but what's best for them."

About the Author

Steve Brown is the author of several historical novels about the Belle family of Charleston. The Belle family saga can be read as a series, or each novel as a set piece about a particular time and place in the history of South Carolina. These stories include the establishment of Charles Town *(The Pirate and the Belle)*, the antebellum South *(The Belles of Charleston)*, the beginning of modern-day South Carolina *(The Old Maids' Club)*, and the beach in the Sixties *(Carolina Girls)*.

You can contact Steve through www.chicksprings.com.

Bibliography

Albion's Seed: Four British Folkways in America
David Hackett Fischer

The Delineator: A Journal of Fashion, Culture, and Fine Arts
Butterick Publishing Company

The Great Influenza: The Epic Story of the Deadliest Plague in History
John M. Barry

Greenville:
The History of the City and County in the South Carolina Piedmont
Archie Vernon Huff, Jr.

Greenville's West End
Judith T. Bainbridge

Greenville: Woven from the Past
Nancy Vance Ashmore Cooper

Greenville County: From Cotton Fields to Textile Center of the World
Ray Belcher

Greenville's Heritage
Judith T. Bainbridge

Hidden History of Greenville County
Alexia Jones Helsley

Historic Greenville: The Story of Greenville & Greenville County
Judith T. Bainbridge

A History of the American People
Paul Johnson

Images of America: Greenville
Piper Peters Aheron

Last Call: The Rise and Fall of Prohibition
Daniel Okrent

McCall's Magazine
1915-1918

The Panic of 1907: Lessons Learned from the Market's Perfect Storm
Robert F. Bruner and Sean D. Carr

Remembering Greenville: Photographs from the Coxe Collection
Jeffrey R. Willis

South Carolina: A History
Walter Edgar

The South Carolina Encyclopedia
Edited by Walter Edgar

CPSIA information can be obtained at www.ICGtesting.com
Printed in the USA
LVOW051445150612

286252LV00001B/7/P